Lorne Greene

Illustrated by Thomas McKeveny

Simon and Schuster · New York

The
LORNE GREENE
Book of
Remarkable
Animals

Published by Simon and Schuster
A Division of Gulf & Western Corporation
Simon & Schuster Building
Rockefeller Center
1230 Avenue of the Americas
New York, New York 10020
SIMON AND SCHUSTER and colophon
are trademarks of Simon & Schuster
Designed by Elizabeth Woll
Manufactured in the United States of America

1   2   3   4   5   6   7   8   9   10

Library of Congress Cataloging in Publication Data
Greene, Lorne.
    The Lorne Greene book of remarkable animals.
    1.   Animals, Legends and stories of.   I.   Title.
II.   Title: Book of remarkable animals.
QL791.G76   813'.01'08   80–11398
ISBN 0–671–24012–9

Acknowledgments

Worthwhile projects are seldom undertaken without the assistance of others, and this book is no exception. I want to express my appreciation to Bill Adler of Bill Adler Books, Inc., who conceived the basic idea, and to William C. Ketchum, Jr., whose research and assistance were fundamental to its execution. It has been a pleasure working with both of them.

Contents

Contents

List of Illustrations

Introduction

It is hard to spend much time around animals without coming to recognize certain traits—the wisdom of the cat, the loyalty of the dog—traits which, alas, seem sometimes more common in beasts than in humans. Yet, like the courage of people, these traits often remain hidden, untested. The animal lives its life and passes from the scene, its unusual qualities never really discovered.

Yet, every so often something remarkable happens to remind us that domestic animals or their wild brethren can, when required, rise to the occasion in displays of heroism, intelligence or endurance fully equal to anything achieved by mankind. The lost dog who returns home across half a continent, the wolf who dies for his mate, the elephant who volunteers to guide his blinded mother, illustrate these remarkable qualities as well as tell a story.

I love animals, and in the many long years during which I have been interested both personally and professionally in the animal world, I have heard many strange but true tales of their exploits. Some of these feats attracted great attention at the time they occurred; others, more obscure but no less interesting, passed without notice except by those directly involved. Yet, all demonstrate an extraordinary degree of heroism, faithfulness, ingenuity and wisdom, especially for animals. As I heard or read each tale, I thought, How could such things happen? How could these seemingly dumb beasts accomplish or endure so much?

After years of observing animals and pondering upon their characters, I still have no explanation for much of what I have seen and heard. I only know that the tales set down here are based on things which really happened and that similar events will no doubt occur again to teach us anew the lessons of courage and loyalty.

LORNE GREENE

Feathered Fury

The young eagle was alone, cold and hungry. He did not understand what had happened, why his mother did not return to feed or warm him with her body. The distant gunshots had, of course, meant nothing to him. How could he know that the Indian hunter who had just slain his mother was even now working his way toward the nesting area. The eaglet was aware only that there had been a change, a change for the worse.

François picked his way slowly through the dense undergrowth of the forest. He knew this area well, for his tribe was native to northern Wisconsin; and the Flambeau River country had always been his home. He loved the rolling lake-dotted hills which were seldom frequented by the white settlers who now owned all the farm and pasture land. True, life was hard in the woods; but, with trapping and hunting and wild fruit in season, one could survive. And now the old Indian was well pleased, for he had killed a great eagle. Its feathers would bring a fine price in the nearest town—enough for salt, bullets and, perhaps, tobacco. He needed little else.

But the red man was not content with the bird which hung over his back, its long wings almost reaching the ground. The eagle had had a nest. If he could find that, there might be more to be gained. When he had first seen the bird, she was circling a hill burned bare by some ancient forest fire. The dead trees on that peak would make a good nesting place. The Indian hurried on.

After a long walk François reached the hill. Several gaunt dead pines clung to its steep slopes, their gray trunks bleached and twisted from the winter winds. His eye traveled up the hill inspecting each bare skeleton. There, on a tree closest to the top of the ridge was what he sought. High in its stark branches was the nest. Was it occupied? He could not tell, but he must find out. Pulling an axe from his pack, François set to work. After a few minutes the tree swayed abruptly and crashed to the ground. The Indian had found what he sought. The eaglet, unable yet to fly, had clung to his home even as it hit the ground and now lay stunned in its ruins.

The Indian reached in to pick him up; but the eagle, shaken yet unafraid, rose to his full height, his naked wings flailing, his mouth open in defiance. The brave started back, his hand reaching for the knife. Then a grudging admiration overcame him. Here was another outcast, a bold renegade prepared to face death in the ruins of his home. Was he not like the Indians? They too fought for life in the remnants of a land which had once been theirs. No, he would not kill this bird. It deserved to live.

François reached into his pack and brought forth a tattered blanket. With a deft movement he flung it over the startled eagle, and in a moment the struggling creature was securely bound to his shoulders.

As he felt the weight of his struggling captive, the Indian recalled all that he had learned of eagles in a lifetime of hunting. Their speed and eyesight were, of course, legendary. The birds could spot a rabbit or a woodchuck from hundreds of feet in the air and could fall upon it so swiftly that the smaller creature was seldom aware of its danger until the long steel-hard talons sank into its back. For this reason Indians had sometimes trained eagles to hunt for them. But the birds were independent, and only a few men were persistent and clever enough to succeed at this task. François had neither the desire nor the ability to train the eagle. But perhaps another might. In any case he felt sure that someone would want the bird and would pay him a good price for it. He turned in his tracks and headed for home.

The eaglet's travels had begun. He was taken to the Indian's home on the Flambeau, where a collar and leg chain were procured and where he was taught to eat small bits of fish and meat, leftovers from his host's table. Then, within a few days, the bird was on his way to the nearest settlement.

Not far from this community lay the farm of Dan McCann. McCann, unlike most other whites in the county, was known as a friend to the Indians; and François resolved, as he had done before, to stay the night with him.

The Indian was surprised to find his usually placid host in a high state of rage and indignation. It seemed that war was brewing. To François war meant the Indians against the white men, and he was debating whether to scalp his host or jump out the window when he was informed, to his great relief, that it was only a white man's war and far away at that. It seemed that some of the states were opposed to others and that already vast armies were in the field.

Moreover, François's friend too would shortly take the warpath. He was preparing to go to Eau Claire, where the troops from Wisconsin were being assembled.

As the two friends talked, a strange scratching sound was heard. Someone or something was seeking admission. The Indian suddenly recalled that he had left the eaglet tied to a tree near the house. Could it have gotten loose? McCann flung open the rough door. There stood the young bird, its cold eyes surveying him.

"My God," exclaimed McCann, "that bird looks as tough as Abe Lincoln hisself! Where'd you get him?" The strange story of the eaglet's capture intrigued the bluff Scotsman, who was already impressed with the creature's self-confident manner. After all, how many recently captured eagles march into a strange house, climb to the highest point and sit there preening their feathers?

As he looked up at the eagle, who stared boldly back, McCann was moved to remark, "He's a real leader, that one. Ought to be a general. In fact, he should at least be in the army. That bird would make a fine mascot for my regiment. You wouldn't be about to sell him, would you?"

François, of course, had had a sale in mind all along, so it didn't take much time for the two friends to come to an agreement. The Indian went on to town a bit richer; and the settler picked up his pack and gun, put the eaglet on his shoulder and headed for Eau Claire.

The rough river town was booming with activity. Hundreds of men swarmed the streets, backwoods sharpshooters in buckskin jackets, rough-handed farmers in denim, brawling loggers from the big rivers, schoolteachers and grocery clerks whose seemingly delicate appearance masked a courage and resolve fully the equal of their more hardened comrades. All had come to fight for the Union, to enlist in the Wisconsin regiments.

McCann stalked the streets with his bird on his shoulder. Instead of being disturbed by the great crowds, the bird was excited. There was something about the turmoil, the ceaseless movement of men and animals that pleased him. And the soldiers sensed this feeling. When McCann enlisted in the Eighth Wisconsin, his bird came along as mascot. He had already been dubbed "Old Abe" in tribute to his stern and haughty visage; and when the trains carrying the troops rolled south, an eagle was among the passengers.

At first McCann found that caring for the eagle was not unlike being a parent. Though wise in its way, it still was young and needed care and attention. The men gladly shared their rations, but hardtack and salt bacon were not an ideal meal

for a bird. McCann found himself bargaining for raw meat at stations along the road and even trying to shoot stray rabbits to supplement the mascot's diet.

And feeding the eaglet required some care. The great bird's beak was like a pincers, and he didn't like to wait. The smell of fresh meat drove him wild, and to offer a piece by hand was to run the risk of losing a finger. McCann learned to place the food in the eagle's general vicinity and then get quickly out of the way. But that too led to interesting and quite unexpected results. Once the eagle got used to picking up scraps, he didn't differentiate between his and anyone else's. More than one soldier had his meal rudely interrupted by a winged visitor who settled heavily on his shoulder and peered down greedily into his plate. Needless to say, the men seldom questioned their guest's right to first taste!

It was a long way from Eau Claire to the war in the South, and many months passed before the Wisconsin regiment saw action—months spent on trains, in crowded, dusty camps and along muddy country lanes. But as time passed, the band of civilians became soldiers; and as they grew, so did their mascot. His plumage came to full feather, and he took to the air, soaring high over the massed ranks below him. He learned to hunt for himself and often roamed far away seeking food.

But, since the business of soldiers is war, there came that inevitable day when they heard in the distance the faint rumble of thunder that turned out to be cannon. They were at last going into battle—somewhere in western Maryland, in an area of hills and woods and farms not unlike Wisconsin. McCann wondered idly if there had been a good crop that year.

For the eagle, there were no such mundane thoughts. His sensitive ears detected the rattle of guns. His nose was tickled by the odors of shot and gunpowder. He surged aloft and swept forward ahead of the advancing troops. Before them lay a thick woods filled with enemy soldiers. Several hundred Confederate troops had broken through the Union lines, and they now lay in wait to ambush the unsuspecting reserves. Disaster threatened. Suddenly a black form plunged from the sky. It was the eagle. He swept over the rebel forces and then, rising swiftly, fled back to the Union lines. As the Wisconsin men approached the woods, they saw the bird swooping about its edge. As the first scouts were about to enter, the bird flew at their faces driving them back. "What's wrong with that crazy eagle?" shouted the commanding officer. "I'll have him shot if he doesn't get out of the way."

At that moment McCann forced his way to the general's side. "Sir," he said, "I think that bird sees something in there. He's never acted like this before." When others agreed with McCann, the officer decided that it wouldn't hurt to fire a few shots into the trees before they advanced.

Of course, the rebels couldn't resist returning the fire, and within a few moments a battle royal raged between the Wisconsin troops and the disappointed ambushers. It was a hot fight but brief. The outnumbered Southern forces soon withdrew, and the regiment advanced into battle. At the general's right there rode, by invitation, McCann and his eagle, the latter having already been awarded the first of his many battlefield decorations!

Abe's feat was naturally of much interest to the soldiers. How had he distinguished the rebels from the Union forces? Was it the difference in uniforms or something more subtle, something akin to that sixth sense by which so many beasts seem to be able to tell their friends from their foes? No one could be sure, but one thing was certain. It was no accident. On several other occasions during the following weeks the eagle spotted enemy patrols and alerted his friends to danger. His value to the regiment and to the Union was becoming clear.

In time, Old Abe became a scourge to the South. Dubbed the "Yankee Buzzard" by his enemies, he was both hated and feared. Wherever the Eighth Wisconsin fought, the bird appeared, and wherever he appeared the Southern cause was doomed. He was considered an evil omen and became so dreaded that rebel marksmen were more inclined to fire at him than at their human opponents. In fact, Major General Sterling Price, commander of the secessionist Missouri State Guards, was once heard to remark that he would "rather kill or capture the eagle than take a whole brigade." Yet the Confederates could not bring their winged nemesis to ground, though they came close —particularly at Vicksburg.

It was late afternoon. High in the air the great bird hung, a gaunt black shape against the setting sun. Below him a dozen Union gunboats slid quietly down the Mississippi. Lashed to the far side of each one was a transport ship bearing hundreds of troops. The date was April 16, 1863. General Ulysses S. Grant was attempting to ferry his army past Vicksburg in order to attack the fortress city from the rear.

For two years the rebel guns at Vicksburg, situated on a plateau two hundred feet above the river, had denied the Union access to over two hundred miles of the Mississippi. Now Grant was trying to take the city, and with him were Old Abe and the boys from Wisconsin.

Just as the sun dipped behind the western hills, the warships came abreast of the city. Startled sentries alerted the garrison, and within moments over two hundred cannon were pouring a hail of iron shot into the passing fleet. The Union vessels replied in kind, and for nearly an hour a furious duel raged between ship and shore. And, throughout the cannonade, despite the destruction all about him, the eagle flew above the Union fleet, his very presence a symbol of hope and an inspiration to courage.

But others also saw the great bird. Confederate sharpshooters posted in trees along the cliff soon recognized their foe and opened fire upon him. The distance was very great and the swooping eagle made a difficult target, but they persevered. Abe became aware of small sounds and faint rushes of air—the passage of bullets. He had come to associate these with danger ever since that day in Virginia when, high over some forgotten battlefield, he had suddenly felt the shock of impact and watched while half his tail feathers floated silently away. He had been frightened then, and he was frightened now.

Turning swiftly, Abe headed away from the city. But it was too late. A bullet struck his left wing, tearing flesh and feather. His flight became erratic. He spiraled slowly down, trying to reach the ships before he crash-landed among the enemy. High in his perch above the city a rebel rifleman shouted with glee and pointed to the descending bird. He quickly reloaded and fired again as others joined in the attack on the faltering symbol of the Union.

But Abe was a hard one to kill. Setting his crippled wings in a glide, he headed for the flagship of the fleet, General Grant's own vessel. The Wisconsin troops saw their mascot coming and knew that he was hurt. They turned their own guns on the Confederate forces and drove the sharpshooters to cover. But almost too late; for as Old Abe settled to the deck of the gunboat, a final shot toppled him. Square in the middle of his great chest the lead slug landed, and he sprawled backward on the wooden planks. Saddened soldiers ran to his aid, but he rose without it. The bullet had traveled too far. Its energy was spent, and it had merely bounced off the eagle's thick feather coat without injuring him. He would fly again. But not at Vicksburg, for even as this drama was being enacted the gunboats and their convoy of troop carriers had passed at last out of range of the enemy cannon. The gauntlet had been run. Tomorrow Grant's forces would go ashore below the fortress city to begin a campaign which would result in its surrender and the eventual end of the Confederacy.

But for Abe, as for many men on both sides, the war was over. He had become marked for death; and as a symbol of the Northern cause, he was too valuable to lose. His chest symbolically covered with medals, he was sent home to serve again, but in a different way. Since his exploits had made him well known throughout the North, Old Abe became a fund raiser. Riding in a special car and wearing a gold medal about his neck, the famous eagle traveled throughout the states of the Union appearing at parades and patriotic events where funds were collected for the treatment and assistance of the many wounded who were already filling hospitals from Maine to Wisconsin.

Even after the war was over, Abe continued to be remembered. When the Wisconsin regiments at last returned home a great banquet was held in the State Capitol building; and the guest of honor was not a politician or a famous general or even a war hero. It was a bird, the first and last time in our nation's history that an eagle was so honored.

And the Capitol building at Madison, Wisconsin, became the renowned eagle's home. A specially designed cage was set up in its cellar, and there Old Abe received each day the thousands of people who came to see him. Those who could not come wrote, and it is said that over twenty-five thousand letters were addressed to the bird in a single year. His portrait was painted several times, his likeness carved in marble, and even his quill feathers were in demand for pens to be used in the signing of important papers.

For over fifteen years Old Abe lived in that cage at Madison, and it seemed that he was destined to end his days quietly, in peace and respectability. But danger and excitement had always been his lot, and fate had saved one final role for him.

Late one night in 1881 a small fire started in the old Capitol building. There were only a few people present at the time, and they were asleep. Slowly but steadily the first tiny flames grew to a roaring bonfire. Papers and furniture were consumed. Thick smoke spread through the building. It appeared that all would perish in their sleep. But again the eagle was equal to the moment. Smelling the smoke and sensing the danger, the ever vigilant bird raised an outcry. Banging his tin water cup against the rails of his cage, he aroused his keeper, who fled to the upper floors alerting others in the building.

As they rushed into the streets, the men called for help; and within a few minutes firefighters were on the scene. By now great clouds of smoke were rolling from the doors and windows of the State Capitol. But the firemen were resolute. Hoses were strung up, pumps were manned and bucket brigades formed. Within an hour the flames had been beaten back. Though badly damaged and covered with soot, the famous old building was saved.

It was then that the fire chief turned to Abe's keeper and praised him for raising the alarm. The man beamed with pleasure, but only for a moment. His face fell. He had forgotten. It had been Old Abe who had awakened him; and in his haste to escape and warn the others, he had left the bird behind.

Filled with dread, the keeper and the firefighters pushed their way into the still smoldering building and down the fire-scarred stairway which led to the cellar. The flames had not reached the cage, but the smoke had. There lay the great bird, dead of smoke inhalation. He had died, as he lived, a hero!

The Sentinel Foxes

Abbot Butler folded the letter carefully and put it back into the black envelope. He felt annoyed and a little bit guilty about his feeling. The Peer of Gormanstown was dead. A shame, of course, but more a shame that the deceased's family expected him to attend the funeral.

The Abbot walked to the window and looked out over the rolling green lawns of Downside Abbey. England was always so lovely in the late summer, and his work was going so well—and Ireland seemed so far away. Still, he could hardly refuse. He and the Peer had been boyhood chums, and they had always corresponded regularly on matters of common interest. But, after all, he hadn't seen the man in a decade and to have to be going to Ireland now . . . But there really was no choice. He would have to ring up the station and see about trains.

Two days later the Abbot sat at the window of a first-class car on the small train which ran from Dublin to Gormanstown. On both sides of the track the rolling grasslands of County Meath stretched away to the horizon, broken here and there by a fence row or a tiny cottage. This was horse country. A pleasant thought crossed the prelate's mind. Perhaps there would be time for a fox hunt. The hounds and horses of Meath were well thought of, and the foxes were said to be a smart lot. One could have some good sport here. But then the nature of his visit once more impressed itself upon him. He frowned at the thought of spending several days holding the hands of spinster aunts and hearing long tales of the Peer's virtues. The Irish were such a gloomy race.

It was late in the afternoon when the train pulled into Gormanstown, and the Abbot was the only passenger to get off. Quaint but undistinguished, thought the Abbot as he observed the cluster of shops and small houses adjoining the old rail station. The Gormans certainly haven't made much of their peerage if this is their market town, and to think they have been here since the fifteenth century.

A one-horse rig was standing near the track, and as the station attendants handed down the Abbot's bags, the driver approached him. "Ye be going to Gormans Hall, sir?" he asked, though it was less a question than a statement. After all, where else would such a well-dressed gentleman be going in this place at this hour?

Gormans Hall stood in a wooded valley some miles above the town. It was old, dating perhaps to the seventeenth century, but well kept; and the lands about gave the impression of being put to good use. The cottages along the road were freshly painted and had bright kitchen gardens. The fields had been harvested, and tall stacks of corn and fodder dotted the barnyards. All in all, an admirable country. The Abbot, who liked neatness and order above all else, began to think better of the local gentry.

After a half hour's drive they entered the woods surrounding the hall. The trees, at least those which could be seen from the road, seemed well kept; and stacks of fresh-cut firewood stood here and there awaiting the woodsman's cart. The Abbot leaned back and let his eyes wander over the landscape. He could see little detail now, for dusk was fast closing in. Suddenly a movement caught his attention. Was that an animal?

Yes, something had moved, just to the right of a large oak tree. He peered into the gloom. A thing like a dog seemed to be crouching there watching them. And it was not alone. There was another and yet another. Odd, how quietly they all sat. If they were dogs, why did they just sit there? Could they be someone's hounds?

Abbot Butler leaned forward to the coachman. "My man, did you notice those dogs back there? To whom do they belong?" There was no response. He repeated the question. Instead of answering, the driver pointed ahead with his whip.

They were approaching the manor house. On each side of the road stood an imposing stone column topped by the figure of an animal, appearing to be a dog. But as the rig drew nearer, the Abbot could see that they were foxes. Foxes, he thought; good news indeed. The Gormans must really love the chase if they had chosen a fox for their family symbol. He could hardly wait to learn if a hunt was planned—after the services, of course.

His arrival at the hall was about as unpleasant as one might expect, given the circumstances. He knew no one, not even the Peer's sorrowing widow. All, even the servants, seemed depressed and silent. They would answer direct questions but appeared unwilling to engage in extended conversation. Still, the prelate mused, dinner and a glass of wine would perhaps loosen some tongues. There were several other visitors, and he could not believe that they would all be so out of sorts.

His hopes proved ill-founded, however. His dinner companions offered little stimulation. The meal was served in an ancient high-ceilinged dining room lit only by candles. At the head of the long oak table stood a high-backed armchair. It was empty. The Peer's chair, no doubt, thought the Abbot. How many of them have sat there over the years? To the left of the vacant chair sat the black-clad widow and below her her daughter and an older woman, the late Peer's sister. On the right were his son and two male guests, both Irish by their appearance. The

Abbot sat across from them alongside another Irishman, who appeared strong and hearty.

The food was tolerable, the wine adequate but the conversation sadly lacking. The women said nothing. The men spoke fitfully about politics, trade and the weather. No one mentioned that which the Abbot most wanted to hear. Could it be that there were no fox hunters here? Yet he thought that he had glimpsed stables in the yard; and then there were those dogs in the wood. Yes, the dogs. He had completely forgotten about them. Perhaps someone here knew whom they belonged to and what they were doing there. The Abbot brightened. He turned to his hostess. "Your ladyship, I saw some dogs in the wood just outside the gates. Are they yours?"

A silence fell over the table. A fork clinked against a glass. The fire crackled in the hearth. Everyone seemed to have discovered something extremely interesting in his plate or on the wall. No one looked at the prelate.

The widow did not speak. After a moment, the hearty gentleman loudly asked the Peer's sister if she would have some more wine. She accepted. Conversation resumed. Abbot Butler was sure that he had said something perfectly dreadful, but he had no idea at all what it was. The meal was finished quickly and in near silence. Everyone seemed to want to leave the table as soon as possible.

Back in his room, the Abbot thought about the evening's disaster. What had he said to give people such a turn? Something about dogs? Yes, that was it. All he had done was inquire about those beastly dogs. Then he recalled that the coachman too had failed to respond to a similar query. What was it about the dogs that had such an effect on people here? In any case, it was an unpleasant situation. Thank heavens the funeral was tomorrow. He could leave in the afternoon.

An odd sound interrupted his reverie. It was like the bark of a dog only a good deal higher. He listened for a while but heard nothing more. The Abbot went to the window and pulled aside the heavy drapes. A cold moon shone on the courtyard. He could see the east wing of the house and to the left a corner of the tiny chapel where the Peer of Gorman lay in state.

All was deserted. Or was it? There was a movement along the far wall. It was a dog again, a small dog; and this one was followed by others; many others. A long line of dogs were trotting slowly across the court. They seemed to be heading for the chapel. A chill ran down the Abbot's spine. There was something strange about those dogs, unnatural.

There was a sudden knock at the door. Abbot Butler let the curtain fall and turned away. He had expected only a servant but was surprised to see that he had a visitor instead. It was the Irishman who had been seated next to him at the table. He carried a decanter of port and two glasses. "May I come in and chat awhile?"

"Yes, yes, indeed," responded the Abbot, who felt now even more in need of companionship. "I have just had a very odd experience."

"Really," said his guest, looking sharply at him. "Let me guess. Have you perhaps just seen another dog?"

"How in the world did you know?" replied the surprised Abbot. "I really don't know what to think now. They seem so odd for dogs, and then what happened at dinner . . ." His voice trailed off.

"Yes, you really stuck your foot into it, didn't you?" returned the Irishman. "Well, it's not your fault. How could you know? I'm Eamon O'Connor, a cousin to the Peer. Sit down and let's have a drink. I'll tell you the whole story. To begin with, those are not dogs you are seeing. They are foxes."

"But how could they be foxes?" exclaimed the prelate. "No fox would come this close to a house and sit and walk in line the way they do."

"Walk in line, you say," responded O'Connor. "So you have

seen them walking in line, have you? Then it has begun again. Let me explain.

"You may have noticed that the house of Gorman displays a fox as part of its coat of arms. One might assume that this is symbolic of wisdom or craft. It is not. It is more on the order of an acknowledgment of family. Long ago, before the peerage was created, the Gormans held these lands as war chiefs. But you English came, and, as has been the case so often since, the Irish lost the battles. The old stronghold which stood on this very spot was burned in the fighting and all the family killed. All save one, that is. A servant, though she was gravely wounded, escaped with a newborn child. That infant was the Lord of Gorman's son, the heir to the lands.

"The old tale says that the woman died in the forest. At least she was never seen again. But the babe, that's a different story. Months later a band of Irish soldiers found the child in the woods. He was alive and healthy; and from his clothing, ragged though it was, they could readily tell that he was the lost heir."

"But what does this all have to do with these confounded foxes?" cried the exasperated Abbot.

"A great deal, my friend," responded the Irishman. "They found the lad in a cave, a fox's lair. The vixen was nearby when they arrived, but she fled. There is no doubt that she nourished him. The boy grew to manhood and in time reclaimed his property. Nothing unusual happened during his lifetime. At least nothing that has come down to us. But at the Lord's death a strange event occurred. Peasants brought word that foxes were appearing in the woods about the hall. The animals moved so strangely and with such purpose that the people were afraid to touch them. After all, they were a superstitious lot in those days. When the story was brought to the Lord's family, the circumstances of his early life were recalled. Wise men advised that the animals should be left in peace, and for a day they filled the woods about the manor. Then, on the night before the funeral, they formed two long lines before the chapel door. There they sat until the body was brought out for burial. Thereafter they vanished as mysteriously as they had come."

"Why, that's absurd," exploded the Abbot. "Do you mean to tell me that live wild foxes are going to form a guard of honor for the Peer of Gorman?"

"They've done so every time a lord has died for over five hundred years," replied his guest, smiling grimly. "I doubt if your presence will change their habits.

"But, of course," continued O'Connor, "we live in different times. Once the presence of the foxes was regarded as a sign of favor and an honor. But for some decades now they have been regarded as something of an embarrassment. After all, how can one in this enlightened age admit the existence of a happening so difficult to explain scientifically. The way the Gormans deal with it is to pretend it isn't happening.

"So, that's your story," he said by way of conclusion. Draining his glass, he stood to go. "Needless to say, it is best not to mention the foxes again or fox hunting. None has been allowed on these lands for five hundred years."

Abbot Butler stood for a long time staring at the door which had closed behind his guest. He could not credit what he had heard, on two counts. First, as a man of God he accepted only miracles of an ecclesiastical nature. This clearly did not qualify as such. Second, as a historian, he accepted as true only that which he had carefully researched. The implications of this second premise troubled him. There was only one way he could verify this story, and it didn't appeal to him.

The prelate looked at the clock. It was past twelve. He pushed aside the drapery and looked once more into the courtyard. Nothing stirred. According to what he had been told, the foxes would now be assembled. If they were not there, he would be vindicated.

Reluctantly he pulled on a sweater and opened the door. The house was quiet as a tomb, he thought unhappily. He went downstairs and out the great front door. It swung softly on well-oiled hinges and did not betray his passing. A chill wind whipped across the courtyard. A bank of clouds partially obscured the moon, and in the dim light the prelate had to feel his way toward the chapel.

It was not long, though, before he reached the corner which he could see from his room. He leaned against the wall listening and breathing heavily. The tiny light which marked his bedroom stood out like a beacon against the dark face of the manor house. There was no sound, yet he felt uneasy.

The Abbot worked his way along the wall of the chapel, his hands against the cold brick. In a moment he would turn the corner and face the doorway. Suddenly the moon was completely extinguished by clouds. He stumbled around the corner and stood clinging to it, his eyes searching the blackness. He could see nothing; but he could feel something, a presence of some sort. He had a strange feeling that he was not alone. An odor filled the air. Where had he smelled it before? In a flash it came to him. The aroma was that of a dog kennel where dozens of animals are confined together.

He drew back, and as he did so something soft brushed against his leg. Back and forth it went, striking him with soft brushlike strokes. The prelate knew only too well what it was. Though he could not see it, he could well imagine the animal whose switching tail was touching him. The Abbot's research was at an end. Using his bedroom light as a guide, he stumbled back across the court.

The next day the Peer was buried. His relatives and the local priest tried hard to ignore the double line of foxes which framed the chapel door. Perhaps if they continued to pretend the beasts weren't there, in a few generations they'd disappear.

In any case, Abbot Butler was not present to share their discomfort. He had taken the first train to Dublin. He never went fox hunting again.

The Tortoise God

The long line of sarong-clad women climbed slowly up the darkened trail. On the slope above them a circle of flickering torches marked the entrance to the god's abode. The worshipers moved quietly and carefully, for each bore on her head a gift: a basket of fruit, a woven mat, a painted carving of the deity.

In front of the cave a group of Balinese drummers beat a rapid tattoo on their log instruments while several dancers swayed enticingly before the black hole. They were trying to draw forth the god. Then, as though in answer to their summons, there was a stirring far back in the recess. Something could be heard shuffling forward. The drumbeats rose to a frenzy. The dancers swirled wildly. Then slowly, ever so slowly, a long neck and reptilian head appeared. A pair of beady eyes surveyed the worshipers. The god came forth. It was a four-hundred-pound Galapagos turtle!

How that turtle got from the Galapagos Islands off the coast of South America to the Dutch East Indies is a long and fascinating story. It all begins back in the 1920s. Early in that decade scientists in the United States became alarmed at rumors of overhunting in the Galapagos, which had long been known as a repository for uncommon birds and animals. It seemed that hunting parties from the mainland, both native and foreign, were killing the rare creatures at random. Particularly threatened were the giant land turtles or tortoises.

An expedition was soon mounted, and in 1924 a ship filled with American scientists returned from the islands with over a dozen of the great tortoises. But, unfortunately, even learned and dedicated men can disagree; and as the ship lay in New York harbor, a dispute arose among the participants in the expedition. While its origin is unsure, the core of the disagreement centered around the disposition of the turtles. Were they to be sold or given to museums, and were individual members of the expedition to have any claim on them? Majority rule prevailed in the matter, but one of the dissidents elected to vote with his feet. In the dead of night he stole from the ship bearing on his shoulders a heavy sack. In that sack was a Galapagos turtle.

Viewing himself, correctly or not, as a fugitive from justice (possession of the turtles is forbidden by federal law), the turtle napper went underground. For over a month he hid out in a small apartment in an obscure corner of New York City. During his weeks "on the lam," as it were, the man's initial fascination with his captive began to wear off. He had not realized how uninteresting it was. For days it seemed scarcely to move at all. It wasn't much of a companion. Nor had he any prior notion of its appetite. The thirty-pound tortoise, though hardly out of babyhood, was a terrible glutton. He swallowed two-pound cabbages as if they were marshmallows and when out of ordinary food would try anything else that was at hand—flowers, magazines, even shoes.

The young scientist's prize had become a liability. He resolved to do something about it. He had a colleague named Dennis, a man who was interested in collecting animals and who had over the years owned a wide variety of bizarre creatures. If anyone could appreciate the turtle, it would be Dennis.

So the deed quickly followed the thought, and within a few hours turtle and owner arrived at Dennis's apartment.

It was love at first sight; though, of course, the tortoise was considerably more reserved, simply indicating his acceptance of the new relationship by settling down on the floor and beginning to gnaw on the carpet. So a deal was quickly struck, and the former owner departed, a bit richer and much relieved.

Dennis and his new pet got along famously. The former was a generous master, providing all that could be eaten; while the latter, for his part, was a most reliable guest. If he was left in a corner in the morning, he could almost always be counted on to be in that same spot in the evening. In fact, except for the slope of his shell, he would have made a fabulous coffee table. But there were some drawbacks. The turtle was growing rapidly. Within a year he weighed over eighty pounds, and, even immobile, he was beginning to occupy a rather large share of the tiny apartment.

Still, Dennis found the giant reptile a fascinating and surprisingly responsive companion. At first, eating and sleeping did occupy the bulk of his time; but gradually Dennis observed a certain broadening of interest. When his human companion came into the room, the turtle would swing his great head toward him as though curious to see what he was up to.

This gave the man an idea. Was the tortoise really interested in him? Perhaps he liked him. Did he too need affection? There was one way to find out. Dennis sat down on the floor beside his guest and ran his hand slowly over his scaly head. The turtle extended his neck. Dennis tickled his chin. The neck stretched further. There was no doubt about it. The turtle really enjoyed having his neck scratched.

It soon became evident that the beast, in his own slow way, was just as affectionate as any cat or dog.

One thing the tortoise would not do, though, was respond to his own name. Dennis had decided to call him "Galloper" in a punning reference to his speed of locomotion and place of ori-

gin, and he tried to train him to come when called. But it was no use. As long as he could see him, the animal would respond to any words he uttered, but once out of sight the man's voice meant nothing to him. Dennis concluded that theirs would have to be a purely visual relationship.

But that in itself was quite rewarding. Man and turtle became fast friends. The animal would sit for hours beside the desk at which Dennis was working, watching him and waiting to be fed or petted. He never showed signs of impatience. For his own part, the human greatly appreciated this silent companionship. It was an ideal arrangement for a writer.

Unfortunately, the situation proved somewhat less ideal for the neighbors. Inevitably they learned of the new pet, and his growth made them uncomfortable. The lady downstairs, listening to the steely rasp of the turtle's claws as it dragged itself across the floor above her head, worried about the day when it would weigh a ton and fall right through her ceiling. She complained. Others complained. The situation was clearly getting out of hand. Dennis decided to move, but where would he go with a companion of this sort and size? Then opportunity knocked.

The 1920s were a time of great change and discovery. Inspired by the writings of Margaret Mead and other anthropologists, Americans were becoming intrigued with obscure parts of the world and the people who occupied them. They wanted information, and they wanted more than just the written word. They wanted to see with their own eyes what was going on in those exotic regions. What better way to achieve this end than through use of the newly developed motion picture camera?

And so it was that Dennis was offered an opportunity to go to the island of Bali in the far-off East Indies to do a movie on the local culture. The people who put up the money thought it was a natural. After all, everyone had heard of those beautiful bare-chested Balinese women and the exotic dances. Dennis, for his part, thought that it would be a nice place for a growing tortoise.

Of course, getting to the East Indies presented some problems. When the passenger ship lines found out that one of the travelers was a Galapagos turtle, they were suddenly booked solid, so Dennis decided to try a freighter. There were lots of small cargo ships that carried people and supplies from one Pacific island to another, and it wasn't hard to find one that would be stopping at Bali.

Some of the crew were a little surprised, though, when they hoisted Dennis's luggage over the side. The second piece up was a big wooden box with five round holes in its base. When they set it down on the deck four legs and a head appeared from the openings, and the box moved slowly away. It was the turtle!

But sailors generally like pets, for the sea is a lonely place, and the crew of the freighter soon became quite fond of the big fellow. It is true that the creature didn't do very much besides sleep in the sun or wander slowly about the decks, but he had a nice way about him and a friendly smile. Also, he was the best garbage disposal unit they had ever seen, much better than the gulls.

After leaving New York harbor, the little steamer traveled south along the Atlantic Coast, rounded the tip of Florida and passed through the Panama Canal. There was a brief stop at San Francisco, then the long trip across the Pacific began. It was a pleasant trip and pretty uneventful until they reached the South China Sea not far from Formosa. This is typhoon country; and sure enough one night Dennis was awakened by the violent rocking and pitching of the ship. He'd been in storms before but never anything like this. He gripped the sides of his bunk and tried to get back to sleep.

Suddenly there was a wild pounding on the door. When Dennis struggled to his feet and opened it, there stood Lou Waters, one of the crewmen. "Dennis," he cried, "we've hit a typhoon and a bad one. We are taking a lot of water across the decks, and I don't know where your turtle is. I hope he hasn't gone over."

"Oh my God," cried Dennis, "let's get up there."

The two men fought their way up the ladder that led to the main deck. There a terrible sight met their eyes. Monstrous waves were surging across the ship's bow, and it was impossible to see more than a few feet through the driving rain and mist. Dennis strained to see through the storm. "I can't tell if he's there or not, Lou," he said. "You know how he likes to sleep in that little sail locker just behind the forward cabin."

"Well, let's go see," replied the sailor.

Waters produced a length of strong rope, and they bound one end of it to the cabin door. Seizing the other in his hands, the seaman waited for the first lull in the storm, then darted across the swaying deck. He made it to a big funnel just before the next wave hit. Tons of water smashed across the vessel, and Dennis completely lost sight of Lou. It seemed impossible he could have survived that. But yet, when the waters subsided, there was his friend, soaked to the skin but clinging bravely to his precarious grip.

The sailor now quickly tied the rope around the funnel: and, taking advantage of the next quiet moment, raced on to the sail locker. Not until he had secured the line to this did he look into the locker. There, sleeping soundly, was the turtle. He seemed oblivious to the typhoon raging all about him.

In the meantime, holding tight to the lifeline, Dennis too had made his way to the sail locker. He agreed that the shellback looked fine, but just to make sure, they tied him to the deck with a spare piece of rope. The turtle hardly budged, just opening one eye and looking at them quizzically as though to say, Why aren't you two asleep like you ought to be?

There was still the perilous trip back across the open deck to be made, but both men arrived safely. The rest of the night Dennis slept fitfully, clinging to his rocking bunk and worrying about the turtle.

He needn't have bothered. When dawn came and the storm passed, a trip to the sail locker revealed that the tortoise had passed an uneventful night. In fact, by the time a sleepy Dennis arrived, the shellback had bitten through his bindings and climbed up on the nearest hatch to take a snooze in the bright sun.

After that, nothing much happened. The voyage continued rather uneventfully, with the ship stopping at one after another of the small ports which dot the numerous islands of the southern Pacific. The days stretched into weeks and the weeks into months. Then one day as dawn was breaking, a great green island was seen far off on the horizon. It was Bali.

The steamer worked its way into the narrow harbor. Dennis and his pet (once again in his carrying case) were set ashore in a strange and exotic land. Palm trees lined the streets, and thatched huts clustered about the open market areas. The people were dark and small, and they moved with a peculiar grace. Dennis was delighted. Bali was all that he had hoped it to be. Now to find a house and get ready to make the movie. He had no doubt that the natives would be delighted to cooperate.

Oddly enough, however, it was now that the would-be photographer's troubles began. The Balinese were courteous and friendly, but they were also not interested in being filmed. There seemed to be some sort of taboo associated with the process, and whenever Dennis would attempt to photograph a ceremony or even a common market scene everyone within range of the camera would gather their belongings and scurry quietly away.

It went like this for nearly a week, and Dennis was beside himself with frustration. It seemed like his long trip had been for naught. In the meantime, however, the turtle had been having a pleasant, if somewhat limited, vacation. He lived in the back room of the large grass hut his master occupied and spent most of his time eating the many varieties of fruits and vegetables which Dennis was able to obtain in this fertile land. Already weighing a couple of hundred pounds at the end of the sea voyage, the shellback continued to grow rapidly.

But, in truth, he was bored. He was fond of eating, but that wasn't everything in life. He longed to stretch his legs (very slowly, of course) and perhaps to visit with his own kind. Confinement to a single small room was not his idea of fun. Dennis, on the other hand, was reluctant to turn his pet loose. After his experiences in New York he did not know how the turtle might be received. They might even want to eat him!

One day, however, all doubts were resolved. While his master was off on another of those futile attempts to film a native ritual, the tortoise discovered a small hole in the back of the hut. Overcome by curiosity, he burrowed into the broken thatch and eventually emerged in the open air.

Just as the turtle's head thrust through the side of the house, a young man, an artist, chanced to come up the path. In his hand he carried a partly completed carving. It was of a turtle. There were no shellbacks in the Dutch East Indies; but centuries before, his people had come across the sea from India, where the creatures were not only found but were also worshiped as deities. No Balinese had ever seen a turtle, but their altars were adorned with replicas of them, and every artist was familiar with the form. Of course, the young man didn't know if turtles really existed. After all, he carved dragons and flying snakes too, and he was certain that there were none of those in the world. Imagine, then, his surprise when he saw the creature of his dreams slowly emerging from the side of an ordinary grass hut.

Cursing himself for his lack of faith, the boy turned and ran back downhill—straight for the house of the high priest. Within a few minutes the aged holy man and his guide had returned to the spot. Since the turtle was moving at his usual rate of speed, he was still there. The priest stared in wonder. There could be no doubt about it. The turtle god, whose very existence he himself in moments of apostasy had questioned, had come among them. It was a great moment.

The tortoise, meanwhile, had taken little notice of his human visitors. He was much more interested in the green things that grew along the path. As he ate, he gradually moved away up a gently sloping hill which led to a small cave, once used as a temple but now abandoned. The priest watched his progress with great interest. Suddenly he spoke. "Behold, he goes to his holy place, the ancient temple of the shelled one which has lain abandoned these many years. There we will praise him. Come, we must make ready."

And with that the old man turned on his heel and hurried back to the village. He wasn't sure that the turtle was really going to the cave, but it seemed like the right thing to say at the time. And, anyway, if he wasn't, he could send out his sons a little later to help the "god" along. The priest didn't know where this turtle had come from, though he expected that it had something to do with the strange American; but one thing he knew: this could make him the biggest holy man in Bali. His head swam at the thought of the gifts and prestige that he could acquire as a result of this fortunate occurrence.

For some years now the priest had observed a dwindling of faith among his parishioners. The introduction of Western ways and technology had caused them to doubt the value of the old beliefs. What they needed was a new infusion of faith, a miracle or two perhaps.

The holy man was no fool. In his youth he had traveled to the mainland and had there seen much smaller turtles venerated for their strength of character, steadfastness and loyalty. He had always suspected that these seeming attributes could be traced primarily to the beasts' stupidity and sloth; but whatever the cause, they were mentioned prominently in the holy scriptures, and turtles when encountered were never molested. They were, in fact, customarily offered gifts of food and flowers.

This gave the priest an idea. If others could have living turtle gods, why should not the Balinese? And not just a god but a shrine and a festival. The opportune arrival of the great beast could lead to a religious revival, and he would be its leader!

And so it was that Dennis had two surprises awaiting him when he returned from his unsuccessful expedition. One of them was the missing turtle, the other was the priest. The holy man was sitting on the stoop dressed in his finest vestments. He rose to greet Dennis. "Blessings on you, holy seer and guardian," he intoned.

"Who, me?" responded Dennis in surprise.

"Yes, you, for you have brought to us across the deep the legendary shelled god of which our histories speak."

Oh boy, thought the photographer, now I know where that turtle went. "But I don't believe he's a god. He's only a—" he began.

The priest silenced him with a sharp look. "Of course he is a god, and you are his priest, second only in power to me, of course. He has come to visit us for a short while, and then he will go away with you. By the way, I understand you have had some problems taking your pictures. As a priest you need only command. The people will regard it as a sacred duty."

Dennis stared at the old man. He thought he'd left all the sharpies back in New York. Well, so it was going to work out after all. He could barely match the priest's perfectly solemn face as he assured him that he regarded it a great honor to serve as the guardian of the great turtle god.

All that evening the lines of people bearing gifts poured up the hill to the cave where the turtle had indeed taken refuge. The drums pounded, the dancers whirled and, almost as though he had been coached, the great tortoise appeared to receive his honors. Dennis, clad in his robes of office, watched it all from a seat on the hill. The turtle would be fed, the high priest would be famous and he would get his motion pictures. The Orient was indeed a remarkable place!

Beware of Raccoon

John Mertens had been walking the trapline since dawn. The snow was knee deep, the temperature barely above zero; still he really didn't mind. There was something about trapping that Mertens liked. Sure, it was cold, hard work and not very rewarding financially; at least not now. The price of skins was way down: too many good-looking "fake furs" and too much pressure from the darn conservationists. Of course, maybe they did have something when they talked about a decreasing supply of fur-bearing animals. Why, he could recall when mink and raccoon were thick all over northern Michigan. Now, you were lucky to get hold of a skunk or a pair of beaver.

The trapper was following a winding, partially frozen river along which most of his traps had been set; and he was watching for the marks he had placed to identify them. It was easy to lose a trap in this country. Under a blanket of snow everything looked pretty much the same, and traps were expensive. He couldn't afford to buy new ones.

Ah, there was one! Mertens noted a blaze chopped on a fallen jack pine and climbed down the bank onto the dark ice at the edge of the stream. The steel chain attaching the trap to the tree had run out taut into the black water. A good sign, he thought. Something had tried to carry off the trap. More than once John had encountered traps occupied by desperate and angry foxes, woodchucks, even squirrels. It was amazing how vicious they could get when caught. But this time when he pulled on the chain, there was only a dead weight; and the animal when he drew it from the water was dead too. It was a raccoon, a big female weighing well over thirty pounds. Good thing, he thought as he reset the trap, there is some market for coon. At least she won't go to waste. Too bad it wasn't a muskrat, though.

He was shouldering his heavy pack when he heard an odd sound. It was a strange whining and snuffling, and it was coming from an old woodchuck burrow under the frozen bank. Mertens knew his game, and he immediately suspected that the raccoon had had offspring and that they were in the hole. He wasn't about to reach in there, though. Even the smallest of raccoons have a fine set of teeth and a nasty disposition. He pulled out his flashlight and shone it into the narrow opening. A pair of tiny eyes stared back at him. Only one, he thought. Well, that's better than nothing. John found a stick and poked it into the burrow. When he withdrew it, an angry young raccoon was clinging to the limb, its teeth firmly clinched on the hard wood.

The animal was tiny, hardly a foot long, and his telltale brown and black stripes were barely discernible. But he clung to the rough stick with a determination which belied his youth, and there was more curiosity than fear in his beady black eyes.

Mertens could not help but admire such courage, still his first thought was to kill the animal. It wouldn't make much of a pelt, but alone the thing would soon starve to death anyway. Then he looked more closely. It was kind of cute, and the kids had been asking for a pet. He knew a fellow down near Detroit once who had tamed a raccoon. It made a good house pet and a fine watchdog too. Even used to scare off the postman. Yes, that was what he'd do. He'd take the little thing home and see if they could raise him.

Well, when John's kids, Ettie and little Jean, saw that raccoon they were fit to be tied. They had had cats and dogs and even a hamster, but this was something else. They fell all over each other setting up a box for him to live in and getting down the baby bottle to feed him.

But, of course, it wasn't all fun and games. Housebreaking that animal was a real problem, and he had a mind of his own too. More than once that winter they had to track him down after he'd snuck out of the box and gone off to hide somewhere in the big Victorian farmhouse. The kids persisted, and their attentions had an effect. It wasn't long before the raccoon stopped trying to bite every finger that came near him and took to following his young masters about the house or crawling into their beds for a nap. He was becoming a pet.

It was Jeanie who really got through to him first. Perhaps because she was more his size, or maybe just because she loved him so much. In any case, the raccoon began to respond to her. She fed him his first bottle and after that the bits of meat which became his steady diet. And it was not long before the little girl could fondle him and even take him into her lap.

However, it was when John found the coon all dressed up in a doll gown and snoozing in Jeanie's baby carriage that he realized she had really tamed it. After that everybody got into the act. They petted the raccoon, stuffed him with food and generally treated him like a pampered child. It was a wonderful experience for the whole family.

Everything, in fact, went very well that winter. The raccoon grew rapidly, and he learned to obey some rules—like staying off the table during meals and out of the pantry at all times. And these are rules, after all, that some children never learn.

But Charlie, as the raccoon was called, did have a major and incurable problem—his curiosity. He could never bear to leave anything new or different alone. He always had to get to the bottom of it. In one case that curiosity nearly proved fatal.

Margie Mertens always did the laundry on Saturdays because

then she could usually count on some help from John. He hated the job, but with this new "women's lib" stuff he felt a little guilty not lending a hand. But this particular day Margie's husband had to take the car into town for a checkup, so she was stuck with the job.

Even with the new automatic washer, keeping the family in clean clothing was a pain; and it was with no great interest or enthusiasm that Margie stuffed the mounds of soiled laundry into the big round Bendix. She'd been at the job about an hour when the telephone rang. Leaving the washer door open, she ran up the stairs. A short time later Ettie happened by, and, like a good child, she shut the door, which of course started the flow of water into the machine.

The first thing Mrs. Mertens noticed when she returned to the laundry room was that the door was shut and that the machine was operating. The second thing she saw was the half-drowned face in the glass viewing panel. There was something in there and it was going around at a dizzy pace. Visions of television thrillers and gruesome reports in the newspapers flashed through her head. She let out a screech and yanked open the door. Just as she had thought, there was Charlie totally bedraggled and looking like he had swallowed half the South China Sea. As it turned out, it was a very good thing that raccoons can survive for quite a while under water and that the telephone call had been a short one. A little artificial respiration brought the pet around, and in a day or two he was fit as ever. However, he never thereafter showed any interest in washing machines and was rarely seen in the laundry room.

By midsummer Charlie was nearly full grown, and he was a rather formidable animal. Weighing over twenty pounds, with a full set of sharp teeth and surprisingly fast for his body structure, he was a match for any cat and most dogs. After a few unpleasant experiences, the neighboring animals came to tolerate if not totally accept him. It was, in fact, not unusual to see several dogs and a raccoon going off on a hunt together. It was also at this time that Charlie first showed his skill as a watchdog.

Northern Michigan in the 1960s could hardly have been called a high crime area; nevertheless, the area had its share of car thefts, vandalism and break-ins. These were not, however, sufficient to overcome the trustfulness and hospitality traditional in the area. So it was not at all surprising that when one afternoon in late September the Mertens family decided to go over to the fair in the next county, they left their door unlocked and most of the windows open. Their only real concession to changing times was that they left their "watchdog"—Charlie—at home. And the only reason they did this was because he was too hard to keep track of in crowds. He was always running off and scaring people.

Anyway, it must have been about ten o'clock that night when they got back, and they were mighty surprised at the crowd waiting to greet them. There was the sheriff and a couple of deputies and several neighbors; and the tale they had to tell was an odd one.

It seems that Lucile Brown, whose husband, Rick, owned a farm just down the road, had driven over about seven to pick up some seed potatoes. She'd seen that the car wasn't in the drive and was just turning around to go back when she noticed another vehicle, a beat-up old green Ford, parked around back of the house. That struck her as odd, since she knew John and Margie didn't have a second car. While she was sitting there wondering about it, the back door to the kitchen flew open and a sort of ratty-looking little man, more of a boy really, came scrambling out. He was kicking and pushing at something hanging on to his pants leg. That something was Charlie.

The kid got to his car all right and inside too, but the raccoon went right after him; and for a while all Lucile could see was arms and legs and tail flailing away inside. Then the door on the opposite side popped open and out came the boy again with the raccoon still on him, only this time it was hanging on to the seat of his britches.

By now Lucile had decided that the unhappy visitor was up to no good, so she backed out of the driveway and headed for home. While she was calling the sheriff, her husband rustled up his shotgun and a hired man and went over for a look.

Well, what they found really made them laugh. There was a dirty-faced kid halfway up the skinny old backyard clothespole with the whole seat of his pants torn out, and a raccoon was running around the base of the pole and jumping up and down like a hound dog who'd just treed a possum.

They just left them both there until the sheriff arrived, and when he saw the sight he started laughing so hard that he could hardly get the cuffs on the prowler.

After that, Charlie became something of a celebrity. He had his picture in all the local papers, was made mascot of the local football team (which was, of course, noted for its defense) and even got to go to the county fair—this time as an honored guest.

All in all, it had been quite a year for the Mertenses. They had acquired both a faithful pet and another daughter; for a third child, Ellie, had been born soon after Charlie came to live at the farm. John Mertens was a happy man as he looked forward to the coming winter and the trapping season.

But that, of course, was before the fire. There had been a real cold snap in early December of '61, and it could not have come at a worse time for the Mertenses. John decided to convert from oil to electric heat, and so he started to pull out the pipes and alter the chimney for the new use. He figured that it wasn't usually very cold this time of year, and they ought to be able to get by with the fireplace and the kitchen stove. Unfortunately, the weather is pretty unpredictable in Michigan, and, instead of the usual temperatures, the thermometer started dipping down into the twenties on a pretty regular basis. After a couple of days of subfreezing weather, Mertens decided that maybe he had just better put those pipes back in and wait until next spring to do the conversion job. He was under a lot of pressure from a cold family, so he hurried; and maybe that's why he made the mistake.

Anyway, he made a beauty. Somehow when he was putting the flues back in, he forgot to insulate a patch of the chimney. So that night when it went down in the teens again and the oil burner started perking away, the heat began to work on the old pine joists which lay close to the base of the chimney. It took a long time, of course, and it was well into the early morning hours when the wood began to char and the first wisps of smoke curled slowly up between the inner wall and the brick chimney stack.

Upstairs, Margie had just given the baby her two o'clock feeding. When she went back into her own bedroom, passing close to the old brick chimney hidden under its many layers of wallpaper, she noticed how nice and warm it felt in that area. What a relief it was to have the oil burner on again. She had really frozen the night before, and the baby . . .

By three, the fire had spread all up and down the walls alongside the chimney, and smoke was beginning to pour out of the registers. It was the kind of thick black smoke that suffocates, and it is doubtful that any of the Mertens family would ever have awakened again had it not been for Charlie.

The raccoon was sleeping in his usual place behind the refrigerator; but, unlike the rest of the family, he was only dozing. Raccoons, of course, are nocturnal; and Charlie had never been able to fully adjust to daytime activity. Now, after a long apprenticeship, he seldom ran about at night, but he didn't sleep well either. So it was his sharp nose that first detected the smell of burning wood and insulation which was slowly filtering through the house.

He was up in a flash and scurrying about the downstairs rooms. Now he could both smell and see the smoke, and he could hear, far away behind the walls, the terrible crackle of flames. Instinctively he knew he must escape. He ran to the door. It was tightly closed. He would have to get someone to open it for him. Someone? Suddenly, he remembered the girls and their parents. They would be sleeping upstairs. That's what people always did at night. He would go get them.

John rolled over in bed, grunted sleepily and swatted at the animal who was tugging at his foot with his jaws. He opened his mouth to scold the raccoon and swallowed a lungful of rancid black smoke. Consumed with coughing, he sat up in bed. He could see nothing, but he could smell smoke and feel a terrible, unnatural heat. He reached for the bedside light and switched it on. Nothing happened. The wires long ago had been burned out.

"Margie, wake up. There's a fire!" he screamed in his wife's ear as he started to drag her from the bed. She was only half conscious, but fear spurred her on; and she too was soon on her feet. They both fought their way through the blackness to the bedroom door, and hand in hand they crept down the hall toward the children's rooms. It was still black as night in the house, but now horrible red lights were flickering here and there as flames began to break through the walls. Outside he could hear shouting. Neighbors were already on the scene. But there was no time now to ask their help. He had to get to the girls.

When they reached the door to the older children's room, they could hear crying. The raccoon had been here too, and both girls were awake. Just as the parents burst through the door, there was a terrible shuddering behind them, and the floor fell away, revealing a pit of fire. Like hell, John thought as he slammed the door.

He soon had a window open and ladders were being put up from the outside. John and Margie knew there was very little time. The floor would go any moment, or the flames would break through the door. Still, their minds were only half on their desperate work, for both knew in their hearts that they had lost their baby.

A few minutes later, mother, father and the two older daughters were huddled under blankets in a neighbor's car. The house was a mountain of flames. Margie was crying inconsolably, while John tried to comfort the terrified girls. There were still no firemen on the scene, but several friends were trying to break into the back of the house. The flames had not yet reached that area, which was directly under the youngest child's room. The men really had little hope, and what they were doing posed a great danger to themselves; but they knew John Mertens would have done it for their children.

They battered at the door with axes and a shovel, and at last it fell in. Covered with water-soaked blankets, the first two rescuers had barely penetrated into the kitchen when the upper stairway fell before them with a roar. But just before it fell, a form hurtled through the air to land with a thump at their very feet. It was Charlie, and in his mouth he bore the baby, burned but alive! The raccoon had performed its greatest feat.

The Misplaced Moose

Ralph Alley rose early that morning. It had snowed again last night, and he knew that the driveway would need shoveling before he could get the car moving.

He was really sick of snow. He could barely stand to look at it now. When, coffee cup in hand, he finally did get up courage enough to stare out the frost-covered kitchen window, his worst fears were confirmed. At least a foot of new snow covered the accumulation already on the ground. What a task, and what a drive it would be to his job in Saratoga Springs.

Alley pulled on his coat and pushed open the outside door. A sea of white spread away on all sides. He picked up the shovel and started. He must have been working for ten minutes or so, head down, shoulders hunched to the task, when he saw it. Just as he raised the shovel and prepared to bite into yet another drift, he noticed something in the snow. It was a hoof print, vaguely like that of a deer but much, much bigger. It was, in fact, over a foot in diameter. Shovel still poised above him, Ralph slowly raised his head, his eyes following the line of tracks. The prints were nearly six feet apart. Only a very large animal could have a stride like that, he thought as he traced the tracks across the lawn, around the garage and off across the field that led to the woodlot.

The man bent now and looked more closely at the nearest track. He noticed that it went all the way down to the frozen ground, right through two feet of snow, crust and ice. Whatever made that must have weighed hundreds of pounds. An odd notion was forming in Alley's mind. He knew it wasn't possible, and yet what else could it be?

Ralph Alley went back into the house. When he came out, he was carrying a rifle and a pair of snowshoes. It was still early, barely light, in fact, but light enough for him to follow a trail. He started off, rifle cocked and ready.

Just as he had anticipated, the tracks led into the woods. Whatever it was, the beast must be huge, for he could see where it had broken off branches six to eight feet above the ground. He moved slowly and carefully now, though he realized that his quarry might well have passed here hours ago. Still, one couldn't be too careful.

There was only about a quarter mile of trees, then he came out on a high bare hill above a swift-flowing stream. He could see the trail going down into the little valley. Had the beast crossed that stream? He tried to see if there were tracks on the other side. As his eyes traveled up the far slope, he detected a movement at the very top of the ridge. Was there something there among the white pine trees? It was hard to tell, for the distance was over two hundred yards, and it was still almost dark. Yet he had seen something. He watched and waited. Then he saw it.

A huge form stepped suddenly out of the trees and towered over the new-fallen snow. Shaggy brown hair covered its body, and a set of antlers nearly four feet across crowned its elongated head. Its eyes were small in comparison to its bulk, and a straggly goatee of lank hair adorned its chin. Had he not been so astonished, the hunter would have laughed aloud at the beast's appearance.

But Alley had little time to observe this strange sight, for even as he gaped, the great head swung slowly from side to side testing the air. Then the man scent was detected. A quick snort of fear, and before its pursuer could react, the behemoth was gone, lost again in the dense undergrowth.

I was right, Ralph thought. I was right, but I still can't believe it. It was without doubt a moose, but a moose here in Saratoga County, New York, within thirty miles of major industrial cities? Here where there had been no moose seen since the mid-nineteenth century? What was going on? Perhaps the animal had escaped from a zoo or circus, but anyway it was about time he called the game warden. Alley shouldered his gun and headed back to the house.

The moose moved slowly through the dense pine grove, stopping now and again to browse on tender branches or edible bark. He was in no hurry, for he had no place in particular to go. Besides, he had been traveling a lot of late. He only dimly remembered the beginning, in early December, when the loggers had come. He had been bedded down in winter quarters, a deep cedar swamp of the sort so favored by his kind. Everything had been ideal. There had been an unfrozen stream, thick brush for shelter and lots of evergreens for browsing. Other moose had been there too, for in winter they gathered for mutual warmth and protection.

Suddenly of a morning, their peace had been shattered by the snarling whine of tractors and the ripping of chain saws. Lumbermen had selected the valley for cutting, and within moments their powerful machines were grinding into the heart of his sanctuary. The sound struck terror into the moose, and he fled west, away from the herd and from his home. He must have run on blindly for hours, for when he finally stopped he was in unfamiliar territory.

He could have gone back, of course, but he had always had a streak of curiosity. He decided to keep wandering on west, following the sun across the sky. Though he didn't know it, of

course, he passed out of his home in western Maine, crossed northern New Hampshire and Vermont and, in early February, reached New York.

That no one reported this animal who weighed nearly a ton and stood seven feet high at the shoulder is somewhat surprising but not really so remarkable. Moose feed and travel mostly at night, and they prefer swamps and thick woods, hardly the type of territory men favor in the dead of winter.

Still, there were those inevitable times when he had brushed the fringes of civilization. A farm boy sledding alone on a high hill outside Conway, New Hampshire, had seen him in a hemlock-filled gulley and had told his parents about the "great big deer." But the hunting season was long over, and his father saw no reason to pursue the matter. An old woman near Rutland, Vermont, found moose tracks in her snowbound garden and called the sheriff. But before he could get there, a heavy snowfall had covered the tracks and there was nothing left to be examined.

Now, however, the moose had been seen and recognized. Though he was not aware of the fact, his troubles were about to begin.

Ralph Alley was on the telephone with the Conservation Department. "I tell you, Warden, I saw a moose. Yes, I know it's 1957, and there haven't been any moose here for a hundred years. But I saw one anyway. How do I know? He looked like a moose. I've seen pictures of them in *Field and Stream* magazine. They got big noses and horns sort of like a deer."

The warden was clearly dubious. The nearest moose were in Canada and western Maine, both hundreds of miles away. Still, Alley seemed sincere. Maybe he had better have a look at those tracks. Reporting that moose had returned to the Adirondack Mountains might just be a feather in his cap.

A few miles away in Greenfield Center, Ruth Bilanski had her driveway all cleared off. She started up her little Volkswagen and pulled out of the yard. She certainly didn't look forward to driving to town in this weather, but she did have that doctor's appointment.

The moose, meanwhile, had decided to seek more shelter. It was broad daylight now, and he wanted to get into a thicket. The valley he was in now looked promising. It ran down into a heavy stand of hemlock and spruce, and there was a little stream too. It was just the thing for a day's rest. However, as he followed the creek down toward the woods, he encountered a problem. A road crossed his path. Above the road the forest was too thin. Below, it was perfect, but to get there would involve crossing that narrow strip. The moose knew about roads, and he didn't like them. In the first place they were open, always a dangerous thing; but more important, he had heard strange sounds on them, roarings and grindings which he assumed must come from some terrible animal he would not want to meet. Still, there seemed to be no other way to reach shelter. He started across.

Suddenly a terrible sound filled the air, and around a sharp bend came what he had feared. A strange squat animal was storming down upon him at a furious pace. There was no time to escape. The moose whirled and lowered his massive horns. He charged his foe.

Ruth Bilanski couldn't believe her eyes. There, charging down on her at full tilt, came the largest animal she had ever seen. She let out a scream and pulled hard to the right. The little car swerved, almost left the road, then righted itself as the great head swept by. As she sped away, Ruth glanced at the rearview mirror. The moose was standing in the middle of the road watching her.

Well, there wasn't much doubt about it now. When late that afternoon Ralph Alley went down to the little general store at Greenfield Center, everybody was talking about the moose. The story of Ruth Bilanski's narrow escape had been on the twelve o'clock news, and the warden had identified the tracks on Ralph's lawn. The animal hadn't been seen again yet, but tracks had been found along the road. They led into the big swamp below Perkins Hill.

Most were talking about the moose, but some were talking about hunting. Sure, the warden had said that there was no moose season in New York and that they'd better leave that critter alone, but to a few men who regularly jacklighted deer and shot grouse out of season that argument wasn't very persuasive. Ralph knew they would go after the moose. He just didn't know when.

Alley was on the phone to the warden again. "Look, Warden, I know these guys. They won't give up the chance to kill a moose, no matter what you or the law says. Hell, I know how they feel. I almost took a shot at him myself. But I feel different now. He may be the only one in the whole state. I don't want to see him die."

The moose, of course, was completely unaware of the turmoil he had stirred up. He had been badly shaken by that experience on the road, but once he got into the swamp he felt safe again. He would spend the afternoon eating and resting; and when night fell, he would head west again, away from roads and monsters.

Unfortunately, though, events were working against the big animal. In an old house south of town two men sat oiling their deer rifles. "What'll we do, Bill?" asked the smaller, a dark man with a hook jaw. "It's almost dark now. We can't get through that swamp at night."

"We're not gonna try," replied his taller companion. "That moose has been moving west all day. I don't know why, but he has. If he moves west tonight, he's gonna come out of the swamp near the old Miller place. We'll be waiting for him."

By dusk the two hunters had established themselves in an old barn overlooking the burned-out Miller house and the edge of Perkins Swamp. Their two battery-powered spotlights were pointed out over the frozen marsh. Rifles in hand, they waited and listened.

The moose was ready to go now. He felt well rested and much more calm. He picked his way through the trees to the low brush that marked the edge of his haven. He felt instinctively uneasy here where there was less cover, though he knew that his movements were shrouded in darkness. Still, it was with some reluctance that he moved out into the abandoned fields that marked the Miller farm.

In the barn Bill suddenly stiffened. "Hush, what was that?" He had heard something, a rustling in the bushes. It was to their left and nearer now. He swung the heavy lights, following the sound. It was coming from the direction of the old chicken coops. He had forgotten about them. They had to get the moose before he got behind those buildings.

"Turn on the lights, Jim," he cried, raising his gun. With a sudden high-noon flare, the spotlights illuminated the old sheds, the field and the moose. He was just passing behind the farthest coop. "Fire," Bill screamed as he sent a round winging after the quarry.

The bright light hit the moose like a club. Surprisingly agile for one so large, he lunged forward out of the glare. As he did so he felt a blast of air across his hindquarters. A rifle slug tore past the base of his tail. A near miss, but a miss nevertheless, and now he was among the sheltering buildings.

Swinging the lights futilely to and fro, the hunters continued to fire, but their prey had vanished. The chicken coops had saved him; and even as they wasted more ammunition, he passed like a ghost into the thick pines behind the barn.

"Blast it, Bill," the smaller man fumed. "We've missed him for sure. What'll we do now?"

"Get out of here, of course," replied his companion. "You never know who may have heard those shots. Maybe we'll get another chance at him, but right now we have to get this gear back in the car and get out of here."

But as it happened, they were a little too late. The warden knew his local poachers well, and he had assumed that Bill and his sidekick would be out after the moose. He had, in fact, been driving around the swamp for over an hour listening for the telltale gunshots. When they came, he knew the direction. It was from the Miller place, and it wasn't long before he reached the dirt road that led to it.

He was just in time too. Down the rutted drive came Bill's car. They had almost gotten away with it. The warden's car blocked their way, and his flashlight illuminated the rifles on the front seat, the jacklights on the back.

"Been doing a little still hunting, boys?" the officer asked, not unkindly, as he motioned them out of the car. "Course you aren't hunting now, I guess, but guns and lights in the car should cost you a pretty penny." The two men looked at each other in dismay. And they hadn't even gotten the moose!

The moose, meanwhile, was making tracks, literally and figuratively. Now thoroughly frightened, he was running just the way he had in Maine when the loggers disturbed his winter home. Except that he was running back east now.

And the animal had good reason to run. The papers were full of the arrest of the poachers, and the news columnists throughout the area speculated on the moose's whereabouts. The great unspoken question was would he reach the safety of the deep woods before someone else got a shot at him.

It was a strange race. On the one hand were those, a great majority, who wished the beast well. These would have fed and sheltered him if they had the chance. On the other hand were the few but deadly enemies of the fleeing animal. To the moose, all were the same. He saw all men's hands turned against him, and the merest sight or smell of human habitations would fill him with terror.

Yet every way he turned he was faced with man or his works. At Stillwater he crossed the great Hudson River on the ice, and a boy with a BB gun filled the air with pellets in a futile attempt to bring him down. Once across the river, he had to cross busy Route 4, and a late-traveling truck driver was astounded to see the huge deerlike creature caught in his headlights. The trucker hit his brakes in time, and watched transfixed as the moose lumbered into the roadside woods.

Once that tale was told, everybody knew once more where the moose was (more or less), and the hunters were out again. Wardens and state police roamed the roads trying to protect the unseen prey from his enemies. Little did they know that he was for the moment quite safe in, of all places, a barnyard.

At Greenwich, up near the Vermont border, Herbert Brown had been awakened along about midnight by cows mooing in the barn. Fearing that a fox or wild dog was about, he decided to investigate. Taking his shotgun, the farmer stole across the frozen field which separated the house from the outbuildings. He peered into the barn. He could not believe what he saw. There, sharing hay with his cattle, was the great moose. Hunger had driven it to desperation.

Brown was both a wise and compassionate man. He had heard of the wandering moose and had observed the frenzy it invoked in some of his hunter friends. It would not be wise to tell anyone of his discovery. He went back to bed.

For over a week the moose spent its days in the deep woods and its nights in Brown's barn. It regained its strength and gathered new hope. Then one day it was gone. The trek had begun again. It was not until he saw in the papers some days later that a moose had been seen in central Vermont that Brown confessed to his neighbors that he had been entertaining the creature recently.

The moose, in the meantime, had learned much on his journey. He no longer ran blindly from houses and automobiles. He traveled only at night, and he crossed roads only when he could hear no cars. As a result, no one saw him again on the highways. But he could be found in barns. At least twice more, in central New Hampshire, farmers found great tracks about their hay ricks. But they had heard no sound in the night, as now the moose did not linger. Somehow he knew he was close to home, and he spent more time traveling and less eating and sleeping.

It was on a morning in late March that the moose reached familiar territory. The lay of the land, the odors in the air, all told him that he was back. He plunged forward through a fringe of low spruce, seeking the shallow creek that led back into his home swamp. Suddenly, though, he was brought up sharply by a terrible and familiar sound. The logging tractor was still there!

As he cleared the last fringe of brush, the animal could see the little tractor far across a devastated field of stumps. The air reeked with gasoline fumes, and the guttural sound of its motor filled his ears. The moose's first thought was to flee just as he had done months ago. He half turned, then a wave of rage swept over him. He would not run again. This was his forest. He would not be driven from it.

Chris Johnson heard nothing, for the sound of his motor drowned out all other noise, but some instinct told him that he was in danger. He glanced hurriedly over his shoulder and could not believe his eyes. There behind him and bearing down rapidly upon the tractor, was a huge moose. Its intentions were clear. It intended to ram his tractor. Johnson let out a howl and jumped clear. He was just in time too; for as the driverless tractor climbed the next hill, the bull moose swept up behind and his great horns toppled it end over end. The moose had taken its revenge.

Lost and Found

Back in the 1920s they used to give out keys to the city of Portland, Oregon—large brass or even gold keys which were regularly awarded to local bigwigs or visiting firemen for some impressive achievement like building a bridge or swimming a river or just not getting caught with a finger in the public till. Lots of men and even a few women got these keys, but only one dog. And there was a lot of controversy about that. Seems like a lot of folks felt that it wasn't quite right to honor a dog like that. Still, that dog had done something pretty remarkable: He'd just walked halfway across the United States with nothing to guide him but his nose and a heart full of love.

The dog's name was Bobby. He was a big hairy animal with lots of Collie blood and a little English sheepdog thrown in for good measure, and he was what people called a "good dog," loyal and loving with the family but death on strangers and strays. Frank Brazier owned him. Frank and his wife, Estele, had a little restaurant in the community of Silverton, Oregon—the "Reo" it was called—and they ran it along with their daughters, Leona and Nova.

Frank had always liked Bobby, especially after he tried to sell him. The family had had a little farm at Abaque, just outside

Silverton, and when they decided to move to town and try the cafe business, they also determined to trade off the young dog so he wouldn't have to leave the country. Well, Bobby didn't like that. He kept running away from his new folks and finding his way to the restaurant. After taking him back a few times, Frank decided that if the pup really liked them all that much he might just as well stay.

And, of course, they all got to like their pet pretty well too. Bobby was the kind of dog that grew on you. He was smart, and he knew his place: never stole food or went where he wasn't wanted. On the other hand, he was very affectionate. One cold night Frank let him up on the bed, and from then on Bobby slept with Frank and Estele. Not that he neglected the rest of the family. He'd follow the girls to school and wait hours just to walk them home again.

So they all settled down in Silverton, and things went pretty well. The Braziers were hard workers, the town was busy and the cafe did all right. So right, in fact, that by the summer of 1923 there was enough money laid by for a trip to see the folks back in Indiana. Leaving the girls in charge of the business, the Braziers and Bobby started east. Roads weren't much good and towns were few and far between, but they made pretty good time; and by August fifteenth they had reached Wolcott, Indiana, only a hundred miles from their home town, Bluffton.

The family stayed a night with relatives in Wolcott, and Frank took the car to a local garage for a look at the motor. Bobby, of course, went along, and that was a mistake. When the big Collie bounded out of the car at the station, he landed right in the middle of a pack of local strays. The fur really flew, and so did Bobby. In seconds he was down the street and around the corner with a dozen mangy curs at his heels.

Frank did what he could. He drove all night, all over Wolcott and the surrounding farmland, calling for Bobby and honking the auto horn, whose distinctive sound had never before failed to bring the dog to him. But Bobby was nowhere to be found.

The Braziers felt pretty bad. They cared a lot about the dog, and it was like losing a child. Still, there seemed to be no hope, and there were people waiting in Bluffton; so the next day the journey went on through Indiana, then back home by way of Mexico and the Southwest. But, of course, things weren't really quite the same.

It wasn't until years later that the family was able to piece together most of what must have happened to Bobby, but it probably went something like this.

The dog was chased a long way by the pack; but he got free somehow, and he went back into Wolcott, arriving long after his master had given up and gone on. For long days Bobby haunted the local garages, clearly hoping that the car and his family would show up again; but they never did, so he started out to find them.

With all our vaunted science, we know surprisingly little about that mysterious force or gift called instinct. We all share it; but most people have lost it entirely, and even in animals it seems dulled by domestication. Bobby's instinct, which was all he had to go on now, was like an old motor. It needed some time to get warmed up. For over three months, from mid-August to late November, he wandered around Indiana, Illinois and Iowa, going north, east, south and west, trying to get his bearings. We know that he covered over a thousand miles, yet he only moved two hundred miles west in all that time, and that was the way he had to go to get home—to Silverton, more than two thousand miles away.

Where was Bobby all this time? Well, after it was all over, a lot of people came forward to explain. After he gave up on the garages in Wolcott, the dog dropped from sight for nearly a month; then one night he appeared on the doorstep of Fred Fiundt, a clerk in Wolcottville, a similarly named town but located way up in the northeastern corner of the state. Months later, when Bobby's story was in all the papers, Fiundt recognized him by his collar and short stub tail. The dog didn't stay long, just about a week, before he headed south. A group of hobos on the White River just outside Indianapolis saw him next. He was swimming the river east to west and coming their way. He was pretty bedraggled by the time he got ashore, and mighty glad to accept a meal of stew and crackers. Bobby hung around a few days, for the 'bos were good men and kind to animals; but he soon felt the urge to move on. Somehow he must have sensed that he was drifting south of the track home, for when he next appeared it was well to the northwest, at a bridge over the Wabash River. A custodian remembered the canine trespasser that he threw into the swirling waters of the big stream, for not everyone was so kind as the clerk and the tramps. But Bobby survived that fall and that swim as he was to survive so many more, and his indomitable will drove him on.

A Mrs. Pratt was sitting under a tree near her summer house on the Wabash when Bobby crept out of the water. She loved him immediately and wanted very much for him to stay with her, but he could not. He was off again the very next day. But, oddly enough, the dog came back five days later for a final visit. At this time it seems clear that Bobby was still wandering, unsure, seeking some clue—in garages, in tourist homes—as to the whereabouts of his beloved family.

He walked across Illinois, meeting no one who remembered him, and entered Iowa, where his next appearance was a real shocker. Frank Patton of Vinton, Iowa, had a car with a horn that sounded a lot like the one owned by the Braziers. Going into town one morning, he sounded it in traffic and suddenly found a dog in his lap. Bobby, mistaking the noise for that of his own car, had leaped right into the vehicle. The Pattons were pretty startled, and they never forgot the bobtailed Collie with the missing front teeth whom they sheltered for the night. In the morning he whined and scratched at the door, and when it was opened he went.

By the time Bobby reached Des Moines, it was November and growing cold. He crept onto a porch and found a young boy sleeping. They got acquainted and both went to sleep, to be awakened in the morning by a very surprised mother. Ida Plumb liked animals, but she really didn't care to have them arrive so unexpectedly. Still, it was a good home and stopping place for Bobby. He must have liked the family, especially the children, for he stayed several weeks. But his mind was always on home. Every day he would disappear for long periods of time. Ida followed him once. He was visiting the local tourist parks.

Des Moines was a dangerous city for Bobby despite the love of his temporary family. Once he vanished for a week to return with his collar gone—replaced by a leather strap and a length of rope. Someone else had tried to "adopt" him. The final straw was the dog catcher. There was a local ordinance against strays, and regular sweeps were held to round up unwanted dogs. They nearly got Bobby. One of the dog catcher's helpers vividly recalls the powerful dog who fought when cornered and jumped clear over him to win his freedom.

Iowa had seen the last of Bobby. Maybe it was the shock of his narrow escape, maybe just that the age-old instinctive machinery had finally begun to function. Whatever the reason, he suddenly saw the way. He bolted west like a cannon shot, running for home. On November 30 he had been in Des Moines. Only six days later he was in Denver with five hundred miles behind him. And he was already becoming a legend. Bridge guards remembered him. A watchman on the Missouri at the Nebraska border remembered the leather strap that broke in his hand as he tried to grab the big dog. He had dived straight into the "Big Muddy," fifty feet below, and he had assumed that the animal drowned among the ice packs and treacherous currents. But Bobby didn't die. He went on. He crossed the Platte River bridge like a ghost, just the memory of a tawny shape fleeing the shouts and the gunshots. He must have stuck to the back roads then, for no one saw him until he turned up in Denver, again finding a kind family to give him food and a day's shelter.

From Denver, Bobby could see the Rockies. Straight across his path they lay, a towering mountain barrier already white with snow. He started up, avoiding the highway and its too curious drivers and the open fields where hunters might lurk.

The leaves had long ago fallen in the woods, and the small game, on which he had subsisted in the plains states, had retired for the winter. He was alone and hungry. At the higher elevations ice coated the rocks and clogged the streams. Soon snow blocked his way, and only by burrowing into it did he survive the terrible freezing nights. Something must have told him that this way was impossible, for he turned back. A week later he was seen in Denver again. His hair was matted and dirty, and he was so hungry he willingly accepted all that was offered.

Then again he was gone, but this time heading northwest and skirting the mountains. Sticking to the high plateau, Bobby worked his way into Wyoming. There he was found outside the door of a sheepherder's hut. The herdsmen were quick to adopt him. Collies have been known as good herd dogs for centuries. They are brighter than most dogs and have an instinct for controlling sheep without attacking the animals. The men weren't about to pass up the chance of acquiring another helpmate.

Of course, they didn't really know if Bobby could do the job, but they found out quick enough; for the night after he arrived, a blizzard struck, turning the high plains into a white nightmare. Great herds of sheep were lost, and Bobby turned out along with the other dogs and the men to try and save them from death by exposure.

An old sheepman who afterward claimed to have been there said that the stray made all the difference. It seems that the lead herd dog got cut off and crushed by the panicked sheep, and that Bobby took his place and saved the herd by turning them from a cliff edge and driving them to safety.

Other such rumors mark Bobby's path through the northwest plains. A one-legged man in a livery stable in western Wyoming claimed that in December a stub-tailed dog came into his barn and stayed for a day or two, eventually leaving with an Easterner who had stopped to buy a horse. The man nearly froze to death in a snowstorm, but when they found him the dog was gone.

Then there was the rancher in the Idaho wilderness who found a half-wild Collie type in one of his traps. He almost killed it for a wolf but was so taken with the dog's ways that he decided to adopt it instead. He had never had a dog before, but he got to like this one so well that when it left after about a week he rode thirty miles into town to get himself a pup. He just couldn't get used to not having a dog around.

Of course, these are doubtful stories, but this much is certain: Bobby forged on. He crossed Wyoming and wandered northwest through Idaho on a path which required him to swim the dangerous Salmon River no less than four times. He navigated the desolate Snake River basin in the dead of winter and, somehow, crossed hundreds of miles of land where his only shelter would have been a cave or an isolated trapper's cabin. How he did it none can tell, but there is no doubt that he did.

In January he reached Oregon and, skirting the impassable Blue Mountains, came into the wide Columbia River valley. There, where the river made a way, the Columbian Highway cut west through the Cascades, and Bobby followed the road. At The Dalles, high in the mountains, he was fed and later recognized. Now he badly needed comfort and shelter, for the trip had left him thin and footsore.

Still, he was on the home stretch. Only a few hundred miles separated him from his goal; and from the mountain heights he could sense if not see the distant Pacific.

He headed down the highway, skirted Portland as he headed south, and stumbled for Silverton only seventy miles away. But he was running out of gas. In East Portland an Irish widow named Mary Elizabeth Smith saw him collapse at her door and dragged him in to die. Bobby now was a terrible sight. His nails were worn down below the hair line. The pads of his feet were gone, leaving only raw bone, and his legs were swollen to twice their normal size. He could not eat, and Mrs. Smith had to give him water with a spoon. Still, she did what she could, bathing his sores and coating his feet and legs with soothing ointment. He seemed near death, yet in the morning he rose and whined for his freedom. She let him go.

It took Bobby two weeks to cover that last seventy miles to Silverton, and by the time he got there he must have been in pretty bad shape. Hunger, fever, exhaustion, whatever it was, clouded his mind, for he went right through town and on out to the farm at Abaque where he had been a pup. His former owners found him there, lying atop the grave of an old dog with whom he had once played. So wasted was he that they did not know him, but nevertheless they gave him food. For a day he lay on the grave, then he rose, his mind clear once more, and headed for Silverton.

Nova, the daughter, saw him first, on a street near the cafe. She couldn't be sure. He was so changed. Yet, it had to be. She called to Bobby and ran for him, but he was gone, tearing across the avenue and in through the swinging doors of the restaurant. Frank Brazier was asleep upstairs—he had worked the late shift—when he was awakened by barking and thumping noises at the door. His wife, not daring to hope, opened it, and a furry body catapulted across the room and collapsed on Frank's chest whining with joy. Bobby had come home. He had traveled better than five thousand miles to make a trip that was a little over two thousand as the crow flies, and he had worn himself to the bone; but it was worth it. The mayor of Portland finally decided to give him the key to the city. None of the other previous recipients had done so much or gone through such pain for love alone.

A Matter of Survival

As Beth opened the bathhouse door, the soft September sun fell once more on the bleached pine benches, the old lockers, the odd bathing cap afloat in a corner. She hated closing up. September was always so lovely, and yet every year it was the same. Just as things on the island began to get really nice—cool nights and bugless days—they all had to go home. And to what? To school. She simply hated school.

The girl's eyes swept the empty room. Nope, it wasn't there either. Where had she put that confounded tennis racket? Beth turned, latched the door carefully behind her and headed back to the summer house.

Unfortunately, she had not noticed Maggie. The cat had been following her as she often did, out of curiosity no doubt, and had slipped quietly in when the door was ajar. The door was now closed again, and Maggie found herself alone. The dark did not bother her, though, and she knew the bathhouse well, having spent many a lazy afternoon there during the long summer. It was warm and inviting. The cat curled up on a bench and went to sleep.

As she lay there, Maggie was the very picture of contentment. Her long silky orange fur (she was part Persian) seemed to glow softly in the dim light, and her plump stomach rose and fell gently as she slept. The cat had been Beth's almost from birth, and she had known nothing but tranquillity and generous meals. Her dreams no doubt contained more of the same.

Meanwhile, back at the house, preparations for departure went on apace. Beth's mother and father probably liked closing time no better than she. For them it meant the end of leisurely weeks on the island, fishing, sailing and loafing. They could now look forward only to a winter working in Chicago. Nevertheless, what must be done must be done.

Howard Roberts shouldered a large suitcase and carried it down the long path that led to the pier where the small motor launch lay. Every year there seemed to be more to bring back: bird houses, pine cones, driftwood, a million items Beth had collected over the summer. And, of course, there were always the cats. By the way, he thought, where are the cats? Maggie and Ralph were always missing when needed. He called to Beth, who was struggling down the trail under a pile of blankets and sheets, "Round up those felines of yours. We'll be off in a few minutes."

Beth scurried through the quiet rooms of the old Victorian house. Where were those cats? They always hid when it was time to go. There went one. She spotted Ralph trying to duck under a rattan sofa. The old gray cat was nearly twelve now, and he had been playing this game for years. Even though she knew exactly where he was, it took her a good ten minutes to corner the elusive pet and to pop him into the carrying case. Then she began to look for Maggie. That presented a more difficult problem.

Maggie was noplace to be found. Beth couldn't understand that. The little female was only two years old, and she had never shown much inclination to stray far from home and the food bowl. Yet she was clearly not in sight now.

After an hour's careful but futile search, Beth called in her parents. Then the quest began in earnest. Howard and Grace

Roberts were thorough people, and they combed that house from top to bottom. There was just no sign of Maggie.

By four o'clock the search had expanded to include the grounds surrounding the cottage. The island itself, being over twenty acres in extent, was too much; but at least they could cover those areas which Maggie was known to frequent.

As he headed down the shore to have a look at the little bay where Maggie had been known to chase minnows in the shallows, Howard reminded his daughter to check the bathhouse. "I've already been there, Dad," she responded, remembering the recent search for the lost tennis racket. There had been no cat in that shed.

It was nearly five when the family gathered once more at the dock. They had spent over three hours searching for their pet, and the train left in forty minutes. "I don't really know what to do now," said Howard. "We've looked everywhere, and I can't afford to miss that train. I have a whole list of appointments scheduled for tomorrow."

"But, Daddy, what will happen to her?" wailed Beth. "We can't just leave her here alone."

"Whatever will happen has probably already happened," responded her father. "You know there are lynx on this island. The Smiths lost their big black tomcat, Tad, to them last summer. He just vanished. And anyway, we can't wait." He turned on his heel and headed for the boat.

Beth's eyes dimmed with tears. She couldn't believe what was happening. Her cat, the only one she had ever had, was gone. For a moment she thought bitterly of her father. How could he worry about trains and appointments when Maggie was missing or hurt or maybe even dead? But her anger passed. That was the way it was with adults. They had their priorities, and besides they never seemed to know how much animals meant to kids. Moreover, she knew in her heart that Maggie was her responsibility. If the cat was gone and she couldn't find her, that was her tough luck. Beth wiped the tears from her eyes, squared her shoulders and marched down to the dock.

It was nearly dark when Maggie stirred sleepily on the bench in the old bathhouse. The family had been gone for an hour. The cat raised her head and looked about. There were long shadows on the walls, and she could both feel and smell the evening damp which was creeping up from the lake.

Time for dinner, the cat thought, and she rose and sauntered to the door. She put her shoulder to it as she had countless times before. Only this time it didn't move. The cat pushed harder. The door didn't budge. All summer that door had swung freely before her. Now it wouldn't move. She felt vaguely uncomfortable. She jumped to a window. Glass rather than the accustomed screen greeted her. Round and round the room the cat prowled. The door and all the windows were closed against her. She was getting more and more hungry, and she was trapped.

The cat's sense of unease was growing. It was too quiet. Where was Beth? Where was the family? Why was she locked up in this room? She had done nothing wrong, at least nothing recently. She had better get out and see what was going on.

Maggie began a more thorough search of her surroundings. She examined the floor, and she found something. In a dark corner, just behind the old footlocker where the life jackets were kept, she found a loose board. The nails had rusted out over the years, and the little cat's strong claws soon forced the rotted wood aside. Now there was an opening, and small as she was, Maggie could force her way through it.

Within a few moments the cat was on the dark wet ground beneath the bathhouse. There were a few inches of space between the dirt and the floorboards; and, alternately crawling and digging, Maggie traversed this until she reached the edge of the building and freedom.

After that it was on to the big house, but she didn't much like what she found when she got there. Locked doors and silence greeted her. It was dark now, but the familiar lights didn't gleam in the big front windows. No smoke came from the chimney. Though she made the obligatory search, the cat knew instinctively that she was alone. Even when she stood on the empty dock and looked out over the dark waters, she did it only as a formality. She had not anticipated finding either boat or family there.

By now, of course, Maggie was very, very hungry; but the house seemed closed against her. Her traditional source of food was no longer available. She had not, however, spent a summer in the woods for nothing. She could hunt; only now it was no longer a game. It was a matter of life and death. The cat turned and melted silently into the dark woods.

There was a spot she knew where the field mice fed among the high grasses of a long forgotten meadow. She went there now and sat quietly in the darker shadow of a thick bush. She waited. In time the grass nearby began to stir gently as though from a vagrant wind, but there was no wind tonight. The cat watched as the tiny wave moved toward her. When it was within range, she pounced. There was a faint squeaking. From the tangle of grass she drew a tiny creature. That field mouse was her dinner.

As the days passed, Maggie became more accustomed to her situation. She missed the family, especially Ralph, in the vague way that animals do; but her life was full enough without them. Hunting had become her major occupation. She grew fat on field mice, and even tried her hand at the daring and elusive squirrels. For a home she had the front porch of the house or, if it was particularly nasty, the bathhouse. All went well at first.

But, of course, it was fall, and the days were growing shorter and the nights colder. Ducks and geese came and went on the lake, and in the mornings Maggie would hear the boom of hunters' guns across the water. Once a boat full of men in heavy coats cruised slowly along the shore. The cat thought about going out on the dock, but something about the way they searched the woods and swung their great guns told her it was best to remain hidden. After that she saw no other humans.

In time the waterfowl all left, as did most of the smaller birds which had frequented the island. The leaves began to fall and in the mornings frost blanketed the ground. In the meadow, mice became harder to find. They were seeking their winter shelters. Even the squirrels became less active. Maggie began to feel isolated.

One morning she awoke early and very cold. There was a thin crust of snow on the frozen ground. It was unmarked by mouse tracks. Winter had come at last. The cat prowled the empty woods. Nothing moved. What would she eat now? Then she remembered the minnows in the shallows. She went to the bay. Yes, they were still there; and though it was cold, tiring work, she succeeded in swatting several ashore. She certainly liked mice better, but Maggie decided that fish would have to do for the present.

But the cold was another matter. The nights were almost unendurable now. Maggie decided to examine the outside of the house more thoroughly. She found what she hoped for. On the north side, a cellar window had been broken; and as a temporary repair Mr. Roberts had substituted a piece of cardboard. Maggie put her head against the flimsy material and pushed. It fell away. The cat entered her old home.

Now it was just a matter of selection. Maggie wandered through the building trying to decide where she would spend the winter. In the master bedroom the closet door was ajar, and in that closet was a great stack of bedding. This was the spot! The cat tugged and hauled at the pillows and blankets until she had shaped them into a suitable nest. Then she went to sleep. That night, for the first time in over a week, she was warm.

And not a moment too soon either, for now it began to snow in earnest. A soft white blanket began to build up around the house; and it was a few days later that she saw the tracks on that previously unmarked surface. She had been to the bay to fish, and on the way back she saw the paw prints. They were catlike but huge, and they paralleled her own trail as though following it. There was an odor about them, somewhat catlike but much more pungent, that she had never smelled before. The animal was big, too big, and it was probably hungry as well. Maggie felt a vague but very real fear. She made a mental note to stay closer to the house.

But circumstances didn't allow for that. The water was freezing in the shallows, and fishing was becoming both unproductive and unsafe. She feared the thin ice which she had to cross to reach the water where the minnows were. Moreover, one day as she fished, her tail froze tight and in a moment of terror she feared that she could not pull free of the ice. When she did escape, leaving behind a thick patch of fur, she knew that she would have to find something else to eat.

But what? The mice and squirrels were well out of reach. That left only the chickadees, and the fat little birds were not easy meat. It took Maggie nearly a day of hard stalking before she finally brought down her first one, and there were few days that winter when she could count on having more than a single bird to eat. The cat found it necessary to spend more and more of her time hunting, farther and farther from home. And that, of course, was the very thing she did not want, for she had never forgotten those strange tracks in the snow.

But it was hard to both hunt and watch for hunters, so one can't really blame Maggie for what happened. It was a dark day with a threat of snow, and the birds were not moving about much. The cat had pursued them deeper than usual into the pine forest. At last, however, in a tiny valley, she had come upon a group of chickadees and had succeeded in capturing one. Now, with the bird in her mouth, she turned to go back.

It was at this very moment that she sensed the presence of another animal. Without even turning, Maggie knew that the lynx was near her. She could smell that strange musky scent again; and as the wan sun broke through the clouds, a very large shadow fell across the snow. The cat backed slowly upon herself, her tail twitching slowly as she prepared for what she knew would be a short and losing fight. Nearby, her great foe crouched upon a log surveying what he perceived to be his next meal.

Their eyes met. The small cat spat. The larger one rose on his haunches in an almost leisurely manner and then, gathering himself, sprang straight upon her.

He never got there, for he was met in midair by a bundle of black fury nearly as large as himself. The tomcat barreled into the lynx with such force that both were sent sprawling. But they were up in an instant and at each other's throats. Over and over the two animals rolled, each trying to gain an advantage. Yet, the lynx was the stronger, and at last he twisted atop his foe and struck for the heart. It was the moment Maggie had waited for. While their foe's full attention was fixed on the male cat, she had slipped around behind the combatants; and now she launched herself at the lynx, her sharp claws seeking for his eyes. The larger animal screeched in rage and pain and fought to free his head.

It was not the sort of meal he had anticipated, not at all. The lynx had had enough. He tore himself free of the snarling cats and fled from the scene of combat.

And so it was that Maggie acquired a mate. It seemed that Tad, the Smiths' cat, had not been eaten after all. He had simply retired to live a hermit's life in the deep woods, reappearing just in time to rescue her. Each cat was understandably appreciative of the other's presence, and after due ceremony they retired to Maggie's home in the linen closet, where they spent a warm and pleasant winter.

In late June of the following year the motorboat once more appeared off Hawk Island. The Roberts family had returned. Though nine minths had passed, Beth had not forgotten her pet. All winter she had suffered nightmares in which she envisioned the various horrible fates to which Maggie might have fallen victim. Now, she thought, I'll have to see if they came true. How could the cat have ever survived the cold of winter and the lynxes?

And yet as they approached the shore, her hopes rose, for her father turned to her and said in some surprise, "Beth, there's something on the dock. Looks like a bunch of animals." Beth and her mother strained their eyes to see what he was pointing at. Yes, there was something there, several somethings, in fact. Could it be squirrels? No, the animals were too large to be squirrels. They looked like cats. Cats! Beth nearly fell out of the boat in her excitement.

And as the boat drew closer, there could be no doubt of it. There sitting on the dock was Maggie, larger and wiser-looking, but still the same old Maggie. And beside her was Tad, and all around them were the kittens, a total of seven in all. Maggie had indeed survived the winter.

The Determined Deer

I first saw the deer in late February of 1968. We had been dropping baled hay from a Conservation Department helicopter for the hundreds of starving deer isolated in the White Mountains north of Conway, New Hampshire. It's rough country up there, mountains, lakes and thousands of streams; practically impossible to get into in the wintertime except on snowshoes or by snowmobile, and we didn't have many of those in the '60s. So there we were in the whirlybird, trying to spot the clusters of starving deer and to put the hay close enough for it to be of some use to them. It was hairy work in those mountains, lots of downdrafts and strong winds. Half the time when we went down into a valley, we weren't sure we would get up and out again.

We had just swung around a big hill after a drop and were starting to climb again when I saw another herd below. They were out on a little plateau almost swept clear of snow, and they'd been eating small fir trees. I could see that for a hundred yards around the young forest was nothing but spindly sticks with a little tuft of green up at the top where the animals couldn't quite reach.

I circled back and came down over while Roger got ready to

make the drop. But as we got in closer, it began to look as though it really wasn't worth it. Of the four deer, three were down in the snow and not moving at all. Fir doesn't provide much nourishment, and it looked like we were too late. But there was one still up, a yearling, and he or she (you can't really tell from up above) was looking at us with something like desperate hope. Well, for a moment I really thought that we should save that food for someone who could make better use of it. But still, even that one deer deserved a chance, so I told Roger to let go. As we rose, I could see the white tail heading for that hay. That deer made an impression on me. His coloration was mighty unusual. He was tan like most eastern deer, but he had a big white blaze right across the forehead.

The deer stood over the torn hay bale eating voraciously. He (for it was a male) was alone. None of the others had followed him; indeed, none could. The food had come too late for them. His mother and two other full-grown deer lay back there on the open plateau, their wasted bodies already vanishing under the snow which had begun to fall again. The gaunt yearling knew that they were dead and that he was alone. These were but minor concerns compared to the need to fill his empty belly.

A while later, appetite temporarily appeased, he became once more aware of the snow. It was falling thick and fast. Though it was barely halfway through the day, it was almost as dark as night. The wind was rising too. Again instinct rose to the surface. Somewhere deep within him the deer realized that he must get to shelter. Without the mutual warmth of the herd to sustain him, he would perish in the open.

About a quarter mile away, down the sloping side of the mountain, there was a deep gully in which a little creek ran. There the fir and spruce trees were taller, and their thickly grown branches formed a sheltering canopy. The whitetail turned and started down. Then he had a thought, a common one for a squirrel or a fox, but a very unusual one for a deer. He returned to the bale of hay and, seizing it by the rope bindings, he began to drag it downhill. It was hard going in the deepening snow, but in some way the deer understood that if he didn't get the hay under cover now he would never be able to find it again.

It was late the next morning before the storm abated. Deep in the spruce grove, the deer was having breakfast. He had spent the night on a warm bed of fragrant needles, and now there was plenty of hay to sustain him for some time. He would stay here until the weather improved. Then he would seek a new herd. Like most of his kind, the yearling needed companionship. Until now he had spent his life with his mother, but she herself had never been alone. There were always other deer, anywhere from a half dozen to twice that number, and all ate, slept and played together. For the most part, the herd consisted of does and fawns, with a single mature male, a buck who ruled over and protected the group. This arrangement seemed quite reasonable to the youngster, and the dim awareness that he was alone filled him with uncertainty.

Time passed. Spring had come, and the deer had grown. Always large for his age and breed, he was now the equivalent of a three-year-old. The stubs of his first horns had appeared, and his coat shone like gold in the warm sunlight as he stood on a high bluff overlooking the meadow in which the herd fed.

All should have been well with the whitetail on that beautiful afternoon, but something was bothering him. There was unrest in the herd. Ever since it had gotten warm, the great buck who ruled them had become more difficult, more possessive of the does and intolerant of the younger males. Only last week he had driven off a three-year-old, and the youngster suspected that his turn would come next. The whole thing was a mystery to him, but he could think of nothing to do about it. He picked his way slowly downhill to where the others were eating.

As soon as he entered the glade, the young buck knew he was in for trouble. The monarch, who had been feeding on the far side of the clearing close to the trees, had now raised his head and was looking intently at him. The whitetail didn't like that look or what followed. For, having examined the youngster at a distance and found him annoying, the larger animal now decided to have a closer look. Shaking his head once or twice, the buck began to trot leisurely across the meadow. As he came, the does and fawns gave way before him like waves before the prow of a great ship.

The whitetail watched his foe come on. He thought of running. That would have been thoroughly acceptable under the circumstances. Yet, why should he? He meant no harm, and he liked it here with the others. He had hated that winter alone in the mountains. He would not give up his family again.

When he was some twenty feet from the youngster, the old buck stopped, lowered his terrible rack of sharp antlers and pawed the ground. Strange guttural cries came from his throat. His small red eyes rolled in his head. He was now thoroughly annoyed, particularly since he had anticipated that his display alone would prove sufficient to send the young buck on its way. But the whitetail made no movement and no sound. He seemed only to wait.

That was too much for the monarch. He let out a great bellow and charged straight for his younger foe. The great horns dipped to strike, but when they came up they were empty! The whitetail had, with astonishing speed and at almost the last minute, simply danced away from the thrust. He now stood a few yards off looking calmly at his opponent. The king of the herd roared in rage and charged again. Once more he found only empty air. Time and again he tried to get his horns into the nimble body which flitted back and forth before him, but his efforts were to no avail. He was dealing with a foe who would not stand and fight and who, worse yet, was beginning to treat the whole thing as a game. For indeed, once he had found that he could avoid the fearsome lunges, the yearling had lost all fear of the larger animal. Now he simply played with him.

After an hour of this the big buck was nearly exhausted. His legs wobbled and his charges were a slow-motion memory of the past. He was beaten and he knew it. Shaking his head sullenly, he turned and went back to his feeding stand. The youngster would stay with the herd.

The summer passed uneventfully. The whitetail ate and grew. He had no further trouble with the old buck, though both sensed that the next spring would bring a final confrontation. That time, however, was now far off. The fall was a much more immediate concern, for with the changing of the leaves there came the hunters.

Deer do not, of course, discuss such things as hunters. They function almost entirely by intuition; yet among the members of the herd there was a clear association between the shorter, cooler days of fall and the menace of the guns. As October passed, the animals began to move out of the low valleys where they had feasted on corn stubble and hay and back into the hidden glades of the surrounding mountains. Feeding, which previously had gone on for most of the day, was now restricted to the early morning and late evening hours; and it was carried out under the watchful gaze of the old buck, who now patrolled almost constantly along the edge of the meadows.

Burt Johnson was a hunter. He found no inconsistency between gunning and the real satisfaction that he derived from piloting an animal rescue helicopter for the Conservation Department. After all, if they didn't feed the starving deer, there might not be any to hunt in the fall. It was, therefore, with considerable pleasure that he rose that gray November morning which marked the first day of the deer season.

Johnson had already selected the terrain for his day's work. Northeast of Conway, near the Maine border, there was an area of old farms. No one worked the land now, but the lumpy, overgrown fields ran back between thickly wooded ridges. Deer living in those trees could feed in the open meadows yet still be within a few yards of the protective vegetation. It was a natural place for the wily animals.

Burt was a still hunter and a good one. He hated driving and the use of dogs to bring deer within range. He liked to match his own wits with his prey; and, perhaps as much, he loved the long hours of solitude which still hunting demanded. This morning he had selected a ridge not far into the woods where there was a stand of beech trees. The nuts would be down now, and perhaps deer would come to feed on them. If not, there would still be the opportunity to sit in the forest, to look and to think.

By the position of the sun, he'd been there about an hour when he saw the deer. It was on the far ridge, partially obscured by pine trees. Though over two hundred yards away, he could tell that it was a spike horn and rather large for its age.

He was a patient man and one who prided himself on having never lost a wounded deer. He despised those who fired at random and at great distance, leaving crippled animals to die and rot in the woods. The young buck was working its way toward him. He would wait for a clear shot.

The deer had wandered away from the herd again. Being outside the control of the old buck had its advantages. He could go pretty much where he wanted to and eat whatever he chose. On the other hand, the monarch had seen a few things in his days, and his insistence on keeping the family together and out of sight was based on a well-founded concern. He had too often heard the shots in the valley and seen the red-shirted hunters picking their way up the brown hills. He knew the death they brought.

None of this, though, meant much to the youngster. He felt the group anxiety that came with the falling leaves, but he himself felt immune to it. He was growing taller and stronger every day, and he had a great confidence in his own immunity. He continued to browse, up over the near ridge and down into a little gully. The beechnuts were scarce here. Perhaps there would be more on that high ground ahead. He began to climb the long leaf-strewn slope.

Burt Johnson settled down over the telescopic sight on his .30-30 rifle. The buck had just gone into a small clump of white pine about seventy yards downhill of him. When the animal came out, he would be in full view. Then he would shoot.

Through the sights everything seemed strangely large. He could see the long needles on the pines and even a tent caterpillar crawling up a tree trunk. Odd that the bug should be out so late, he thought; but then, it had been unusually warm this fall. He eased the gun stock against his shoulder. It should just be a few moments now.

Then the deer showed up. His long neck and small rack of horns appeared from behind a gnarled and blackened pine. Johnson's finger tightened on the trigger as the cross hairs of the sight settled directly behind the animal's ear. He was facing back downhill; but then, and quite unexpectedly, the deer turned his head and looked straight at him. Burt gasped in surprise. A long white blaze ran down the center of the deer's forehead. There could only be one mark like that. It was the yearling that he'd seen on the mountain last winter.

One thought after another raced through the hunter's head. Wasn't this what it was all about? That deer would have starved to death. Now he would be harvested and utilized. But he had saved him. Could he now kill him? What a loss that would be. But would it? That deer would be dead of natural causes within a few years anyway. Still, this wasn't just any deer. He had once made a conscious decision, at some personal risk, to save him. Was he now to make a conscious decision to destroy him? No, he was not. He lowered the gun barrel and stepped out into the open. The deer gazed at him in seeming fascination. He had never seen a man before, though he knew they spelled danger. Yet, he could sense that this one meant no harm. For a long minute the two looked at each other across the rock and grass and brush, then the animal turned and faded out of sight amid a stand of tall beech. Burt settled back against his tree. No doubt there would be another buck along in a while, and if not, there were always the woods and the quiet.

Winter followed the fall, as it always does; and it was a bitter winter too. There wasn't much snow, but there was a good deal of ice and bitter cold so that the ground was covered with a slick sheet through which the deer were constantly breaking, cutting their legs on the sharp edges. Finding food was less difficult than usual, as the snow cover was not deep; but movement of the herd was greatly hindered, and this was a serious matter, for the dogs were about. Packs of them—some wild, some just on temporary leave from their farm homes—began to harry the immobilized deer. In deep snow they would have presented little problem, but on ice it was a different matter, for dogs could skim over a crust through which the sharp-hoofed deer broke.

It was early January when one of these packs found the whitetail's family. The deer had yarded up in a hemlock grove above a deep and open stream. There was sufficient water and food, and each day was pretty much like all the rest until the strays came.

The young buck had been off on his own as usual, and he was some distance from the others when he heard the baying and yelping of the dogs. It was a sound he knew, though he had not as yet associated it with a particular animal. Nevertheless he sensed danger and headed immediately back to the deer yard.

When he arrived he found chaos. Nearly a dozen lean and hungry curs were swarming about the frightened herd. The great buck was defending a small group with his horns, but the rest were scattered and the dogs were tearing at them. A doe was already down, the tendons in her legs torn beyond repair. Not far away another was trying to save her fawn from a murderous attack by two great hounds.

The youngster hit the pack from the side and quite unawares, for they had assumed that all the deer were cowering before them. He burst from the woods within yards of the hounds, and before the largest could turn he had it on his sharp horns. In an instant the eighty-pound beast was high in the air, its red blood spraying the snow. Even before that dog had hit the ground, the buck was on his second foe. The hound bared its fangs and leaped, but the deer turned with the speed of light and presented his iron-shod heels. There was a terrible cracking sound as they smashed into the dog's head. The hound fell to rise no more.

The buck turned, seeking new foes. There were none. The pack had had enough; silent now, the dogs slipped back into the forest. The youngster moved slowly into the center of the herd. As he did so, the old monarch gave way and stepped aside. There was no doubt now who would leave in the spring.

The rest of the winter passed uneventfully. The buck watched over and protected his family. Burt Johnson flew his missions of mercy, dropping hay to those deer so unfortunate as to have been caught out in the cold without provisions. The man thought occasionally of the deer; the deer thought not at all of the man.

Then it was spring, and with the coming of warmer weather Burt learned that he had a new and rather unusual assignment. He had been directed to do a bear census. It seemed that the Conservation Department wanted to get some idea of just how many bear there were in the state of New Hampshire, and bear were a lot easier to count when asleep than when awake. Burt, who knew that black bear where notoriously grouchy in the spring, thought the whole idea was pretty silly; but what could he do? It was all part of the job.

Anyway, a few days into April he found himself back up in that country north of Conway. It was the same area he had hunted last fall. Only now he was hunting bear and without a gun. He knew the area, though, and he had a pretty good idea of where some bear dens might be. He was right. Too right, as it turned out.

Burt was uneasy as he climbed down into the narrow gorge. He remembered a big cave here, a natural spot for bruin; but he didn't much like the location or, particularly, the timing. It was getting along into April now, and he had already found a couple of dens empty, their inhabitants risen to go forth in search of food and mates. He hoped that this bear would still be asleep. It would be difficult to get out of the way quickly among these sheer walls.

The deer too was uneasy. Though he did not know it, he was maturing, and strange feelings stirred within him. His new rack of horns was sharp and tall, and he longed to test them against something. Yet, the old buck had left without a struggle, and he had no one to challenge him. So he came away alone; and now he was climbing a long narrow valley, a vague curiosity pushing him on.

It was just when the deer reached the head of the glen that Burt slipped. He had been clinging to a branch about eight feet above the cave mouth when the wood suddenly gave way and he tumbled headfirst to the ground. Fortunately (more or less), his fall was broken by the large furry object onto which he fell. It was a bear.

Bruin had just awakened. He was understandably outraged by the blow on the head and the presence of the man on his doorstep. He decided to take immediate action. Snarling with rage, he reached for Burt, who was now trying to crawl away from his three-hundred-pound adversary, much like a beaten wrestler seeking the safety of the ropes. But fortunately for the man, the bear never reached him. He was distracted by a new sight.

Standing at the edge of the clearing before the cave was a large deer. He was looking at the man on the ground. He seemed to be deep in thought. The bear reared again. His cave was becoming a tourist attraction.

The bear rose to his full height and glared at the deer. When he had met these creatures in the woods before, they had fled before him. No doubt this one would too. Then he could get on with the business at hand.

But no, the buck did not run or even flinch at the sound of the bear's voice. Instead he lowered his head and began to paw the ground in an expression of unmistakable rage. The old bear couldn't believe his eyes. Such temerity. He would soon put an end to that. Forgetting about his human antagonist, the bruin surged forward again—at his new foe.

The two animals met about halfway and with a terrific impact. The deer was set back on his heels, and the bear reeled from the blow. They looked at each other with new respect. After that the fighters became more cautious, with the deer trying to get his horns into the bear, and the latter trying to get past those deadly rapiers so that he could sink teeth and claws into the unprotected hide.

The struggle went on for quite a while, long enough for Burt to get to the side of the gorge and to drag himself up it to safety. Once there, he turned to watch the climactic moments. The bear had decided to end things with a mighty rush. Gathering himself, he leaped straight upon the deer. The buck never wavered. He took the charge upon his great horns and, recoiling like some powerful spring, hurled the bear back again. When he landed near the entrance to his cave, bruin suddenly remembered that he was not yet thoroughly awake. He decided to go back to sleep, and with hardly a backward glance he darted into the den.

The great buck slowly turned away, and as he did so he swung his horns high in the air, almost in salutation to the man who stood above him on the rocks. Burt Johnson was not even very much surprised this time. There was the white blaze. Now they were even.

The Seeing-Eye Elephant

It was early afternoon, and the hot sun beat down on the dense jungle. Rain had fallen the night before, and a curtain of steaming mist rose from the dank vegetation. Astride the lead elephant, Singh cursed the heat, the jungle and his life. In the village it was deemed an honor to be a mahout, or elephant driver, but those who saw it thus never had to experience the reality of the job—the danger, the hard work and the sheer boredom of hours spent sitting atop a plodding beast.

Still, for a poor man, the son of a tenant farmer, it was a good position. At least, unlike his father and brothers, he did not have to toil fourteen hours a day for a cruel landlord. Singh had known long ago that the rice fields were not for him, so when the recruiter for the timber company came looking for men to train as drivers, he jumped at the chance.

True, it was risky work. Only a week ago a young man whom he knew had been trampled by his mount. Elephants were strange that way. Once they had accepted a driver they would generally remain loyal to him for life. Yet, there were those all too frequent instances when the beast would turn, often without warning, on his master. Sometimes it would happen because the animal was frightened by a snake or a thunderclap. Sometimes it was because the mahout was too cruel or too demanding. But there were also those times when no explanation for such behavior sufficed.

Singh shuddered. It was not easy to spend most of one's waking hours aboard a multi-ton monster whose personality you could never really hope to understand. But it was a job, and a far better one than he could ever have hoped for. He had been able to save a few rupees, and he had a fiancée. In a few years he would be well enough off to marry, something his older brothers had little hope of. But he earned his money. This trip proved that.

For three days now he and his fellow handlers had been pushing their mounts through the rain forest of southeast Burma on their way to an isolated logging camp where the animals were needed to move and stack heavy timber. The work they had to look forward to would be hard—it always was—but the journey was proving far worse. This area was little traveled, and the trail was narrow and overgrown. Great trees crowded against the path, and heavy creepers hung everywhere, ready to trip or snare the passing caravan. Time after time Singh had to swing his sharp machete against vines which barred the way. It was hard and tiring work.

Nor was it any better for the elephants, particularly the calf. Plodding along behind his mother, he tried to figure out what it was all about. Up until now his life had been a pleasant one, consisting mostly of long days spent eating, sleeping or wallowing in muddy streams. True, he had had to follow his mother to the fields where she was made to lift heavy burdens, but this did not really seem to concern him; and anyway that sort of thing might even be fun. This walking, on the other hand, was certainly not fun. It was torment. With his shorter legs he had trouble keeping up, and his thinner skin suffered cruelly from the thorns and swarms of biting insects.

The trailside vegetation grew ever more dense. The handlers were beside themselves with rage and exhaustion. It seemed that they were being swallowed up in a sea of green. Some of the creepers were as strong as heavy rope, and it took several blows to sever each one. Others were soft and pulpy, but when they were cut, floods of liquid poured forth covering man and beast. The drivers were soaked and miserable, but still they persisted; for at the present pace the caravan would be able to reach the logging camp before nightfall. None of them relished another night on the road.

The elephants too were tired, and they were hungry as well; but, responding to the mahouts' prodding, they plodded onward. The calf's mother, Mahoo Nee, or Fire Opal, was just behind Singh's lead elephant, and her child followed close behind her.

It was because of this that the tragedy occurred. As the band entered a shallow valley through which ran a muddy creek, they encountered a particularly thick stand of creepers. The vines hung across the trail like a curtain. The drivers rose to their feet atop their swaying mounts and began to hack a tunnel through the suffocating blanket of vegetation. Swinging wildly to his right and to his left, Singh failed to notice that among the familiar vines there was a new arrival, a thick purple-black stem which exuded a strange odor. It was the Ban Lai, a rare plant whose acid juice was dangerous to both man and beast.

Thinking only to rid himself of the clinging strands, Singh slashed through the black vine. As the severed trunk snapped back, a thick spray of orange liquid filled the air. The man was fortunate. The mist settled behind him. Fire Opal was not so fortunate. Her eyes were filled with it. She felt a sudden searing pain, and a darkness settled over her.

Singh knew something was wrong when he heard the elephant's frightened, agonized trumpeting. He turned about in time to see Fire Opal rear into the air, unseating her handler, then stumble uncertainly off the trail. The confused animal went but a few feet, though, before she ran head-on into a giant tree. She reeled back and stopped with her head down and her trunk swinging nervously from side to side.

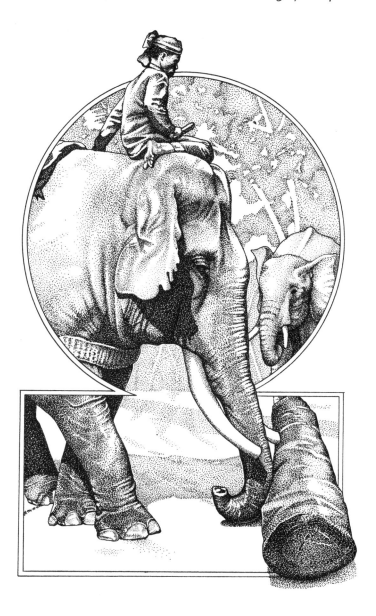

The other driver was now on his feet, unhurt, so he and Singh hurried to the elephant's side. She was calm now, for the terrible pain had abated. Singh approached her head and gently pulled it about so that he might look into her eyes. He found what he had feared. Fire Opal's once brilliant brown eyes were white and glazed. The acid had burned all life out of them. The elephant was completely blind!

The mahout felt a sinking sensation in the pit of his stomach He had just cost his employers several thousand dollars and himself a job. A blind elephant could neither work nor live. It would have to be destroyed—probably right here in the jungle, for there would be no way to get the beast to the logging camp.

Just then they noticed the calf. The little one had been left behind when his mother bolted off the track, but he had followed her into the bush and now stood nearby. Instead of trumpeting with fright as the men would have expected him to do, the calf was grunting softly as though talking to his mother. She responded in a similar tone; and then, as the handlers watched in puzzled silence, the young elephant worked his way to his mother's head, backing gently up against her. For a moment they stood thus, then the calf grunted again. Fire Opal slowly raised her great trunk and placed it gently on her son's back, linking herself to him. Without another sound, the calf turned and headed back to the trail with his mother following close behind. Fire Opal had a guide!

Singh was amazed. He had worked with elephants for some years now and knew them to be extremely social beasts. One of the reasons that they could be trained to do so many things was that they seemed to take pleasure in working together. True, they were intelligent, at least to the extent that they could follow a series of simple commands; but the real key to their effectiveness was the way handlers could get two or even three elephants to tackle the same job as a team. That was something one could not expect from most animals.

Yet, what had happened here was quite different. The calf

hadn't been trained to aid his mother. He was doing so on his own, apparently out of love and concern. Sure, Singh had known that elephants "talked" to each other. Their everyday activities were accompanied by a medley of sounds ranging from low rumbles of affection to great bellows of rage. But he had never dreamed that they could convey such precise instructions. Clearly, he thought, as they once more set off down the jungle trail, there was much that he had yet to learn about his giant companions.

It was a strange caravan that arrived that night at the logging camp. The workers were accustomed to seeing mother elephants leading their offspring, but never before had they seen a child leading his mother. As they watched the animals go through their evening routine, they wondered ever the more, for the calf seemed capable of solving every problem presented by his mother's lack of sight. He led her to the water for a bath, then stood between her and the treacherous depths, sounding a warning whenever the blind elephant strayed from the shallows. When it was time for dinner, he guided her to the fodder and, using his trunk as a broom, swept the food into a pile which Fire Opal could easily find and eat. At bedtime a gentle nudge and a few soft sounds were all that were necessary to tell the older beast that she should follow her son to the bedding grounds in a thick bamboo grove.

The manager of the logging camp, an Englishman named Duncan, watched all this with great interest. His first instinct upon hearing of Fire Opal's plight had been to order her death. If she could not work, she was of no value. Moreover, if the calf were to serve as her guide and constant companion, his labor too would be lost. On the other hand, the manager was not without compassion. The loyalty and skill of the young elephant moved him. He had also to think of the workers. They were visibly touched by what had happened. Some were even saying that a god inhabited the body of the young elephant, whom they had now christened "Bo Lan Pya" or Guide Man.

The Seeing-Eye Elephant

Duncan had been long in Burma, and he knew that the natives regarded elephants with much greater respect than was usual among white men. To them the animals were much more than just beasts of burden. It was not by accident that the temples of Southeast Asia were frequently decorated with carvings and sculptures of elephants. It would not be wise to tamper with such beliefs.

As he pondered his dilemma, an idea came to the manager. Three creatures were involved in this: the blind elephant, the calf, and Singh, whose carelessness had caused it all. Why not let them see if they could work things out.

Accordingly, on the following day Duncan called the mahout to him. "Singh," he said, "as you know, your error has caused us great damage, and by rights you should lose your position. But you are a good man, and I would not like to lose you. I have observed the calf with the blind one. It occurs to me that if he can help her to bathe and to eat, he may also be able to assist her in working. If you and he can do that, Fire Opal will live and you will stay with us. See what can be done."

The task which had been set was not an easy one. It was one thing to lead the elephant to water and to food, quite another to guide her in the complex maneuvers required to drag logs from the forest and to stack and lift them into the waiting railroad cars. While he did not exactly despair of his chances, Singh regarded them as rather slim.

Nevertheless, the chance must be taken, and that afternoon the three went into the forest. Great trees were lying all about, while in the distance could be heard the sound of saws and the crash of falling timber. Many of the fallen giants were three or four feet in diameter. Only an elephant could move them. Fire Opal was trained for the task. Now she must be trained to do it in the dark.

At Singh's command the great beast knelt so that he might mount. Before doing so, however, he drew close to Fire Opal's ear and spoke softly. "Great one, this is the test. Blind though you are, you must do your job. Otherwise you will die, and I will starve. Let us begin."

The mahout doubted that the elephant could understand what he had said, yet she did understand simple commands; and he must not miss any chance. Bringing his mount to her feet, he applied his goad to her ear and attempted to direct her to the first log. Fire Opal did not move. Instead, the elephant swung her head about in a bewildered manner, as though searching for the elusive timber. She could smell the log and understood what was expected of her, but she could not manage it without sight. For over an hour the handler tried to guide his beast to the log. He stroked her, encouraged her, threatened her; but nothing seemed to work. Singh was at the edge of desperation, not only for himself but for his companion as well. In his way he loved the elephant, and the thought of her impending doom filled him with misery. But what could he do?

All this while the young elephant stood quietly by watching everything that took place. He was not old enough yet to have been trained to work with logs; yet somehow he understood what was required. As Singh sat dejectedly upon Fire Opal, the calf moved forward. Trumpeting softly, he nudged his mother until she was alongside the log. Then, at his direction, she placed her trunk on his back; and he in turn circled the end of the log so that her trunk was now across it. Feeling the wood, the older elephant knew what to do next. She quickly wrapped her strong trunk about the piece of timber and lifted it free of the ground. The rest was comparatively easy.

Guide Man simply nudged his mother along the trail to the timber yard and, when there, guided her trunk with his own, so that she might place the log atop the correct pile. It took quite a while to perform this chore the first time the elephants did it, but by evening the team was working nearly as fast as the other beasts.

Through all this, Singh was simply a passenger. He had no real part in the work, nor would any man again, as far as Fire

Opal was concerned. Her son was now her mahout. Singh was not a particularly religious person, but as he watched these amazing proceedings he could not help but wonder at what some of his companions had said about the calf. Had a god indeed taken possession of Guide Man's body?

Whatever the cause, Singh's problem was solved. The next day when the manager watched Fire Opal and Guide Man perform, he declared that they were entirely acceptable. True, the arrangement was a somewhat unusual one; but if the work got done, that did not matter. And besides, now he did not have to lose a good handler. Moreover, the workers were delighted with the whole thing. They were able to witness what they regarded as a near miracle; and he, Duncan, was now regarded as a kind and fair master, a thing which could only result in greater production. All in all, things had worked out quite satisfactorily.

And so for nearly two years the elephants worked together, both in the forest and along the river where they dragged logs from the sandbars where they had been stranded during the high waters of the monsoon season.

Each time Singh came to the camp, he was delighted to learn of some new achievement, some further proof of Guide Man's remarkable ability. But the young animal was maturing, and that bothered him. He spoke of his concern to the manager.

"Mr. Duncan," he said one evening, "you know Guide Man has never been trained, because he could not be taken from his mother for long enough. He is now nearly full grown. I fear what may happen to him when he hears the mating calls of the wild ones out there in the jungle."

Again Duncan was equal to the moment. "We could chain him, of course," he replied, "but we have never done so, and I do not want to start now. He is a rare beast. Let us see what he does."

The truth was that Duncan had developed a great respect for Guide Man. He had seen a lot of elephants in his time, and he admired their intelligence and loyalty. Yet, he had never known a beast such as this. The calf's seeming ability to solve problems and his evident desire to care for his blind mother moved him greatly. Though he did not share the natives' superstitious awe, he still felt somehow caught up in a fateful chain of events. So far, Bo Lan Pya had met every challenge without human advice or restraint. Now he and his handler would soon see if the calf could overcome the greatest challenge of all, the mating call.

Nor did they have long to wait. It was only a few weeks later that the trumpeting of the wild herds broke upon the camp. The elephants stirred; but they had been trained not to heed the call, and they soon returned to their work—all but Guide Man. For a long time he stood apart listening to the sound, his ears high and a wild look in his eyes. Once he started and seemed to be on the verge of moving into the bush. Singh watched him with growing anxiety. But just then Fire Opal, impatient to get on with the work, called to him. Without hesitation, he went to her side. His love and sense of duty were greater than his mating instinct. Duncan had been right.

The following year the monsoon rains came early. Along with the other elephants, Fire Opal and Guide Man were brought out of the forest and put to work at getting stray timber off the sandbars before it was swept away and lost in the rising waters.

This work was hard but not nearly so complex as delivering logs to the railroad; and, in fact, Fire Opal, once she had been properly placed, could do most of it by herself. Since he was not needed by his mother and as he was not yet strong enough to work by himself, Guide Man was often left to his own devices. He would rest on the bank or walk along the shore until his mother's call would summon him to her assistance.

On one such day the young elephant ventured farther than usual from the work area. He crossed the river at a shallow ford and wandered down along a high bluff from where he could look out over the stream and the camp. He liked the view, and he drew closer to the edge—closer than he should have. Unknown to him, the rain-swollen waters had undercut the bank. It could not bear his weight.

Fire Opal, working where she had been left on the far side of the river, was the first to realize the danger. Even before she heard the terrified high trumpeting she could sense that her child was in danger. Though she could not see, the great elephant's head turned unerringly in his direction, and she too let loose a great cry. Plunging neck deep in the boiling waters, she tried vainly to find a way across the river. Only when she felt her feet slipping on the edge of a sheer drop did the blind mother draw back. Meanwhile, Singh, lying half asleep in the shade of a banana tree, had heard the terrible sound and sprang to his feet.

Far across the water he could see the bank and the elephant upon it. Even as he watched, a huge chunk of the brown earth separated from the rest and arched out over the void. Upon that mass of soil stood Guide Man! Slowly, almost gently, the cliff face slid fifty feet down into the swirling brown waters. The young elephant, still calling for help, went with it. For a long time the man watched the river, but Guide Man did not appear. He was gone as surely as if he had not existed.

Singh went to the manager. "Mr. Duncan," he said, "with the calf dead I fear for the mother. How can she survive without him?"

"She will," responded Duncan. "She must. She has worked long enough, and I am content to retire her. But I want her alive as a memory of this remarkable occurrence. See that she is fed and watered regularly and that she wants for nothing."

But the Englishman could not understand the true nature of the relationship between the two great beasts. Though she was fed and given water and even bathed regularly, Fire Opal steadily wasted away. She stood for hours with her head pointing out over the river in the direction from which the last call had come. And one day they found her, dead, lying down, with her head still pointing toward the river.

Duncan couldn't understand it. How could an animal die just like that when she lacked for nothing? It appeared that he had been wrong and Singh had been right. Well, he thought, in Burma two out of three isn't so bad.

Sailors' Luck

The low barroom was dark and full of tobacco smoke. Fog pressed against the windows and swirled in each time the outer door was opened. A few men, sailors by their appearance, sat or stood at the long scarred bar. One of them, an old salt in a ragged striped shirt, spoke.

"Aye, Nils, it's a stroke of luck that we got the black cat with us. We hauled more sardines this trip than I've seen in thirty years. She's lucky, she is."

"Sure she is, Helv," responded his short fat companion. "It was a good day for us when we found her on the dock. Didn't want to come along, though. Remember how she scratched you? I still wouldn't trust her to come back if she got over the side."

A little farther along the bar a younger man, also a sailor, was listening intently to all that was being said. What he heard gave him great hope. He was a deckhand on the *Sultera*, an old coaling vessel, and he had known just such a cat as they were describing. In fact, he and his mates were looking for her. It had been here in Liverpool a few months ago that their mascot had vanished, and since then everything had gone wrong. They had sheared a propeller on a rock outside Dover harbor and lost two weeks' time; they had a man drown in the Channel; and now they were stranded in port, losing time and money because their shipment of coal had been delayed.

If this was their cat and if he could get her back, things were bound to get better. The listener buried his nose in his beer and waited. After a while the older men finished their drinks and turned toward the door. The young sailor followed them.

Staying in the shadows, he trailed the somewhat unsteady seamen back to their vessel. It was a large Norwegian fishing trawler. As the two mounted the gangway, the man who had followed them stood perplexed. Should he ask them about the cat? Should he try to go aboard and see for himself? He quickly rejected both alternatives. This crew knew the value of their mascot. They would not give it up. No sense letting them know that there was any danger. There had to be a better way, and he would find it. For now, he would go back to his ship.

Early the next day two men installed themselves in the old warehouse that stood next to the pier right where the Norwegian boat was docked. They were the young sailor and a companion. From a second-story window the conspirators could look directly across the dock onto the deck of the fishing boat. For a long time they watched. Then they saw what they had hoped for. Coming out of the main cabin was a coal black cat. Her long silken fur glittered in the sun. She moved with an air of complete authority, as though she owned the boat—which, in a sense, she did.

A man came from the cabin. He carried a bowl of milk, which he placed before the cat. She sidled slowly up, took a couple of tenative laps, stretched as though from boredom and walked off.

"It's her, Jim. I knewed it was," crowed the young man to his companion.

"You're right, Ben," the latter responded, "but how do we get her? The gangway's up, and there's men on deck."

"I've got a way," responded the first, and he drew forth a

long piece of string and several small rather smelly pieces of chicken liver. "You know how Cat" (for that is what they had always called her) "loves liver. If we can get her attention, she will come for it."

One of the chunks of meat was quickly tied on one end of the string and then lowered out the window till it hung about a foot above the ground. There it jiggled seductively up and down. Waiting until all was quiet on board, Ben then gave a long low whistle.

Cat was familiar with the sound. She had heard it many times before. Her head came up. Her ears twitched. She recalled how the cook on the *Sultera* had whistled when he called her to a meal of fresh chicken livers just up from the galley. The thought of liver pleased her greatly. She was sick to death of salty sardines and powdered milk. She wanted something different.

The sound had come from a building next to the ship. The cat slipped quietly across the deck. She was thinking of taking a walk, but she knew that her shipmates wouldn't like that. For some reason, once she got aboard a vessel no one wanted her to leave. She would have to be careful.

Arriving at the railing, the feline deserter looked up and down. Through the window of the warehouse she could see the dim outline of a face. She thought that she knew that face. Then she noticed something else. There was a string hanging from the window. Her gaze followed it down. No mistake about it, there was a piece of liver at the end of that line.

Down in the boat's galley the cook placed a couple of sardines on a plate. That cat had been getting fussier and fussier. He had better take her some fish and keep an eye on her too. They would be sailing in a day or two. Wouldn't pay for her to take off.

Cat looked down. It was only twenty feet to the dock. All was clear. She jumped. Once on the ground, it was only a moment before her sharp claws were closing upon the dangling liver. She pulled it to the dock and, just for old times' sake, began to worry it a bit before eating. For once she had forgotten her usual caution.

Suddenly, a pair of work-worn hands closed upon her. It was the young seaman. He had hidden within the building and pounced on her unawares. The cat spun in his arms, her claws ready to strike. Then she relaxed. It was her old friend from the *Sultera*. He had raised her from a kitten. She would not harm him. Besides, she was getting used to being kidnapped.

At that very moment a cry rang out aboard the Norwegian trawler. "Let loose that cat, you thief." A sailor stood on the deck and two more were running forward. Jim burst through the door of the warehouse. "Come on, Ben, run for it or we'll lose the cat and get a beating besides. Those guys are mad."

But the trawler's gangplank was raised, and by the time their pursuers were able to lower it the culprits had vanished. Liverpool was a big place, and it would take a long time to find the right ship. The Norwegians started looking.

A while later, back on the *Sultera*, a band of happy crewmen surveyed their prize and heaped praise upon her rescuers. They were not at all surprised when the captain burst into the room to announce that the owners had gotten coal. The shipment would be loaded that evening, and they would be on their way with the dawn. Yep, Cat had brought them back their luck!

For Cat, the *Sultera* was a familiar place. Unlike humans, she remembered nearly everything of her life from its earliest moments, and she clearly recalled lying newborn against her mother in a dark corner of the galley. Something terrible was happening at the time, something which she learned later was a storm. The ship lurched and bucked, and the man who tended her and her mother had the smell of fear about him. He felt that the ship would surely sink that night. Of course, the kitten knew nothing of that or of the fact that within a few hours of her birth (the only black cat in a litter of four) the storm had unexpectedly abated.

It was neither to Cat's fault nor credit that the superstitious sailors believed her birth had brought them salvation, but that belief changed her life. From then on, it's true, the voyage did go remarkably well; and as each good thing happened it was chalked up to the presence of the tiny black kitten.

That this should be the case was in itself rather strange, for traditionally black cats had been regarded, and particularly by seamen, as harbingers of bad luck. Yet among the priests of ancient Egypt they were highly prized; though, of course, the sailors knew nothing of this. Their faith was based more on coincidence than anything else—a strong feeling that a coal black cat was appropriate to a coal carrier and the fact that among the countless kittens which had been born aboard this ship, Cat was the first black one. And, besides, hadn't Hans, who had been with her at the time, sworn that the weather had begun to change only after her birth as the last of the litter? Whatever the case, luck did seem to follow the little animal.

Accordingly, it was quite a shock to the crew when, after two more good voyages, Cat fell into the hands of the Norwegians. But they had her back now, and they planned to hang on to her. Once more, of course, they failed to reckon with the ingenuity of their feline guest.

Cat did sail again on the *Sultera*, but it was not a happy trip for her. She felt that the food had deteriorated, and some of her favorites among the crew had departed for greener pastures. So when the ship next made port, she started looking for a way out. Unfortunately, the crewmen had anticipated this. They decided to lock their feline good luck charm below decks for the duration of their stay in port.

And so the cat found herself a prisoner in a small windowless room. She continued to be well fed, of course, but that was not enough. She had to get out. Ceaselessly the cat prowled the cubicle looking for a weak spot. The door was the only one, and each time it was opened a burly man blocked it. Still, Cat had an idea.

The next time the cabin door opened, the sailor gasped in amazement. The cat was gone! Nowhere in the bare room could it be seen. He rushed in to search. That was what Cat had been waiting for. Down she dropped from the ceiling, where she had been clinging to a pipe, right onto the seaman's shoulder. In a twinkling she had kicked off again, sinking her claws into his flesh as she vaulted out into the passage.

Now the race was on. The cat flew up the corridor pursued by one, then two, then a half dozen men while cries of "Stop her," "She's loose" and "Get that cat" rang out. As she darted up the stairs that led to the main deck, the cook suddenly appeared before her. He bent to grab her. Cat sprang straight over his head and out the porthole. She streaked to the edge of the ship, then stopped in shock. They were not at a dock. The vessel was moored to a buoy two hundred yards offshore!

The cat turned at bay. Her back was to the rail. Before her a dozen men advanced in a semicircle, cutting off all escape. She knew that they meant her no harm, but they wanted to deprive her again of her freedom. Cat couldn't stand that. She looked at the black waters below and then at the pursuers. She made a choice. Without another backward glance the cat vaulted the rail and plunged into the sea.

The crewmen gasped with shock and surprise. What had they done? They hadn't dreamed the animal would do that. They only wanted to preserve their luck. Now, they looked at each other in horror. What sort of ill fortune would come of this?

Meanwhile, Cat was swimming slowly toward shore. The bay was bitter cold and stank of oil. The black greasy substance clung to her fur and dragged her down. She had seen the land and knew its position, but it was a long way off. Progress seemed unbelievably slow. There was a strong offshore breeze, and that too worked against her. She did not know how long she swam, for time lost all meaning. All that mattered was to keep afloat.

After what seemed a lifetime the animal saw something ahead. It was a sea wall. The cat swam slowly along the barrier seeking a way up. It was eight feet high and of smooth concrete. There were no handholds. Cat was growing weaker. The chilly water and her swim had taken their toll. She did not quit, but she swam ever more slowly. Completely waterlogged now, she began to settle beneath the surface.

Just at that moment, a round net engulfed the surprised feline, and she was lifted clear of the water. An old crab fisherman had seen her plight and had rescued her.

Once she had recovered from her brush with death, Cat was quite delighted with the new state of affairs. She was washed, cleaned and fed and spent the next week lounging by the fire in the fisherman's home. This was a tiny cottage right next to Liverpool's public pier, and from the window the animal could see all that took place on the dock. She was very content, and it was possible that Cat might have spent a long time with her rescuer, but one day when she looked out the window, she saw a great ship tied to the pier. It was a passenger liner.

For a long time Cat sat looking at the liner. She could tell that it was something very different from the vessels with which she was familiar. Certainly the people going aboard were very different. Instead of baggy pants and Levi's jackets they wore furs and fine suits. They looked terribly clean. Cat wasn't sure, in fact, that she would like them at all. Still, she sensed adventure beckoning.

The next afternoon about four the cat observed a change in the activity aboard the big steamship. People were moving faster. Steam was rising from the funnels. Lines were being loosened. She knew these signs. The ship was getting ready to depart.

Cat went to the door and mewed loudly. The old man let her

out. He loved his own independence, and he respected that of others. He would have loved to have a cat but only of her own free will. He watched as his departing guest moved swiftly down the dock. Where was she going?

The fisherman sighed softly. It was not easy living alone, and he had done that for a long time now. Once there had been his wife and the family and a whole raft of pets. That had been in the upcountry overlooking the coastal town. They had had a garden and an orchard and animals everywhere—horses, cows, ducks, chickens, dogs and, naturally, cats. But that was long ago. His wife had died, the children had grown up and gone away. The big house was filled with too many memories. He had sold it and moved down here by the quay where he could watch the ships. Though never a sailor by trade, the fisherman was fascinated by their life. But the harbor was no place for pets, at least not for most. Still, he could have had a cat. There were enough of them around. But he had this thing about independence. He didn't want to take one. That was like putting it in prison. He wanted a cat to come to him. And one had. But now it seemed to have changed its mind.

Cat arrived at the gangway at just the right moment. It was empty. All the passengers were aboard, and the sailors on watch had gone off to file their clearance papers. The cat took a final look around, then up she went. Off to sea once more!

For Cat, this voyage proved a mixed blessing. The crew knew of her and adopted her gladly. The passengers, on the other hand, were generally indifferent or downright hostile, particularly after one found Cat sampling her salmon salad! As a result, Cat had to spend most of her time below decks. On the other hand, the food was remarkable. Things she had never dreamed existed, like turkey and swordfish, found their way onto her plate. Still, she had no special protector, and she missed sleeping in a sailor's bunk. Then one night she met a friend.

John Nolan was not aboard the steamer of his own choice. He had taken the job as a steward as a last resort after going through a sizable personal fortune, two marriages and the patience of most of his friends. He was really down on his luck, and the cruise hadn't helped. He hated catering to the fat old women who reminded him of his mother, and he didn't appreciate being ordered about by people whom he had always regarded as his inferiors. As a result he drank too much. All in all, it was a dreadful business, and, like his life, he was thoroughly sick of it.

So late one night, fortified by a half quart of Scotch, John stood at the rail debating the wisdom of casting himself over the side. He saw no reason to go on as he was, and swimming away into the night appealed to him.

Cat saw the man standing there in the darkness and felt herself strongly drawn to him. She could feel that something was wrong, though she didn't know what. "When in doubt, purr" was her motto, so she slid up to Nolan and began to rub against his leg. John looked down. He'd never had much interest in cats; besides, he was about to jump overboard. Still, it wouldn't hurt to take a few minutes to pet her. He bent over, and the cat went boldly up to him and thrust both forelegs about his neck. The man was quite taken aback. This cat clearly liked him. As he sat on the deck with Cat cuddled in his arms, John gradually lost interest in suicide. That night Cat slept on his chest. She had found her protector.

Nolan wasn't sure exactly what had happened. He certainly had never had much interest in cats. But this one had shown an interest in him, had, in fact, saved his life. He wondered idly if the animal had guessed his intentions. How could she have? Still, there was a funny feeling that he owed his feline friend a very heavy debt. But it was even more than that. The near suicide had been a turning point. Up until then everything in his life had taken a downward course. He had had everything and had tossed it all away—his life had merely been the last thing left to dispose of.

Perhaps now he could start fresh. And why not? At the moment he was like the cat. He had nothing but his life and his wits. She seemed to do very well with just these, perhaps he might do as well. At least he could try.

After that things went much better. John Nolan stopped drinking and began to put his life back together. Cat, under his supervision, got to spend more time in the sun; and even the grumpy old ladies said that she had become much better behaved.

But like all cruises this one came to an end. The ship returned to England. John Nolan was met at the gangway with news of hopeful business prospects. He must go to London immediately, and that was no place to take a cat. And as for Cat, she too was glad to make a change. There were other ships to travel on and other seas to sail. She started on up the pier with an expectant look in her eyes.

And that expectation was fulfilled. In the next five years Cat became a legend on the high seas. She shipped to Australia on a grain carrier and came back with a load of cattle. She went to the Americas and to Alaska with a scientific expedition. Everywhere she traveled the crews had safe and prosperous voyages. No one wanted to be without their feline good luck piece.

But Cat's life became hectic. Only when aboard a ship on the high seas was she able to relax. In port she was in constant danger of being kidnapped by other crews or imprisoned by her own. She was nine years old, and it seemed like she would always be on the run.

In fact, just such thoughts were going through the cat's head one bright morning as she darted through the Liverpool streets. She had come in from Japan on a big merchantman and had escaped by hiding in a bale that was being unloaded. But she was seen as she crawled out, and now half of the ship's crew was after her.

As she ran, Cat caught glimpses of familiar sights. Half the ships tied up along the wharf were ones she had sailed on.

Most of the sailors now pursuing her had done the same thing before when they had served on other vessels. Would it never end?

Then up ahead Cat saw a small house. She knew that house. It was the home of the man who had saved her when she was drowning in the bay. Putting on a great burst of energy, Cat surged ahead of her pursuers and vaulted through an open window. It was as though she had dropped from the face of the earth. The sailors had no idea where she had gone.

That night when the old fisherman came home he found Cat purring contentedly in his favorite chair. She had come home to stay. For the rest of her long life she was quite content to sit at the window and watch the ships come and go. Cat's sailing days were over.

The Vagabond

George Bircher was first to arrive at the post office that snowy February morning. There were already ten inches on the streets of Albany, New York, and the blizzard was expected to last out the day. Delivering the mail sure wasn't going to be much fun, thought George as he tried to force open the snow-clogged front door. He had the key in the lock and was just turning the knob when he heard something, a sound like a bark but tiny and weak. It was coming from under the stoop.

The old postman got down and peered into the hollow space beneath the steps. Sure enough, there was something there. A pair of eyes peered out at him, and before he could withdraw his head, a wet tongue slapped across his face. It was a dog—a little brown and white mongrel only a few weeks old.

It's funny how things work out. If it had been a nice day or if someone else had already been in the office, George would probably have sent that pup on its way. But in this weather and alone as he was, he just didn't feel like doing that. The dog was obviously abandoned, so Bircher picked him up and took him inside.

Once there, George got a closer look at his new charge. He really wasn't much to look at, though, just a knob-kneed street cur with a funny little switchy tail and a nose a bit too large for his face. But there was something distinctive about the dog's eyes. They were deep brown and big, so big that they dominated his whole face, and they had a look of real intelligence.

Bircher knew right away that this was no ordinary animal. He was destined for big things, and big things need big meals; so the postman got out his tin lunch pail and rummaged around till he found a bit of cold steak. The dog accepted his offering gratefully, and a firm friendship was established.

George decided to call the dog "Owney" because he didn't have any owner, and little Owney really took to being a postal employee. He wasn't much of a watchdog, but back in 1888 there wasn't much need for watchdogs anyway, so Owney spent most of his time just being a companion to all the men who worked in the post office.

He watched them sort and pack mail and do the innumerable chores that always need doing around any office, but as he grew older the dog became more and more interested in the actual process of mail delivery. At first he went on all the routes and followed the postmen around the streets of Albany watching them drop off and pick up packages and letters.

And the dog must have figured out that the mail came and went in bags and that these bags arrived and left on trains, because by the time he was a year old Owney was meeting every mail train. He seemed to enjoy the process of loading and unloading; and naturally he got to know a lot of the people who worked on the trains.

Then one day Owney just vanished. The postmen were quite worried, because he had never been away before. They imagined all sorts of terrible things and checked all the obvious leads—the dog pound, the police station and so on. There was no sign of their pet. But three days later a train from Buffalo, out in western New York, arrived, and when the mail bags were unloaded, so was Owney. It seems that he had hitched a ride with the train going west and had gotten off in Buffalo to

spend a couple of days visiting with the local postal workers. Then, when he was ready to return, he hopped on an Albany-bound train and came home.

Well, of course, the mail car workers had liked having him along, for they are ordinarily a pretty lonely lot, and they hadn't been too keen about letting Owney off at Albany. George figured then and there that if the dog was going to start traveling, everybody had better know where he belonged, so he got him a collar with his name and the Albany post office address on it. Then one of the other men had an idea. If their pet was going to travel around like a letter, he ought to get canceled like one. So they attached a card to his collar with a request that all the postal employees he visited stamp it with their cancellations. This way the men in Albany would know where Owney had been.

After that first taste of traveling there was no stopping Owney. The dog became a familiar figure all up and down the New York Central railway. And the idea of a cancellation card proved to be a good one too. Postmen were delighted to add their stamps to it; and, strangely enough, Owney seemed to treasure the mementos. In fact, after a year or two he had so many of the cards hanging from his neck that he could scarcely raise his head. But he never abandoned the collar. He learned how to remove it while at home or on a train, but as soon as he reached a new destination the dog would wriggle back into his neckpiece so as to be ready for the next cancellation.

By this time Owney was becoming something of a celebrity. News of his visits was carried east and west on the mail trains, and soon postmasters throughout New England were eagerly awaiting his visit or petitioning Albany to arrange one. In a way, George and his friends kind of liked this. It was nice to own a famous dog; it gave them a kind of reputation too. But, on the other hand, they really didn't get to see much of their pet anymore. Owney was away almost all the time, for his travels had broadened.

George was the one who suffered the most. After all, he'd raised the dog from a pup, fed him, bathed him and nursed him through a dozen illnesses. Now the mongrel was so busy riding mail cars that all George got to do was wave or throw him a bone as he passed through. The postman sort of accepted that, though. After all, Owney was like a son to him, and wasn't that what kids did when they grew up—go off and leave you? Still, he couldn't ever quite get used to it. Just didn't seem normal for any animal to travel the way that one did.

By 1892 Owney had covered most of the Northeast and was tackling the transcontinental lines, riding the rails to the farthest parts of the nation. Even the Postmaster General down in Washington had heard of him; and, in 1893, Owney was awarded a lifetime pass entitling him to a free ride in any U.S. mail car.

But nothing seemed to satisfy Owney. He was truly the canine version of the great American hobo, and he seemed determined to ride just as far as the rails would take him. In 1895 they took him to Alaska. The dog had reached Portland on one of the first trains to cross the northern Rockies, and he was hanging around the post office there when the mail started to go out to the Alaskan Territory.

Alaska was a long way off, and the way there was pretty rugged, for the land was just being opened up. The line was just a little single-gauge one, and the cars weren't much; but, of course, Owney didn't know anything about this and probably wouldn't have cared if he had. All he knew was that here was a train he hadn't traveled on going someplace he hadn't been to. So naturally he climbed aboard and headed north.

The dog's arrival in Fairbanks precipitated a wild two-day celebration, for the new city was teeming with hundreds of gold-seeking prospectors, and they delighted in crazy antics—like entertaining a famous dog. By the time Owney started south again, he was so fat that he couldn't squeeze into his beloved collar. Well, this would never do for the prospectors. A bunch of them just went out and bought the dog a new one complete with diamond-studded gold nameplate!

New nameplate and all, Owney went on down to Seattle and found his way to the harbor. Who knows what the animal thought when he looked out across the vast Pacific Ocean? One thing he must have sensed was that he couldn't go any farther west by rail. He had just run out of track. But there was an alternative.

Lying alongside the dock in Seattle was the S.S. *Victoria*, outbound in a week for the Orient. Naturally the *Victoria* was carrying mail; so when the roustabouts started bringing mail aboard, Owney joined them. The ship's officers took one look at his collar and knew they had a famous guest aboard. They had heard of the traveling dog and were delighted to think that they could have him as a passenger. It was in Asia that Owney really came into his own. In the United States dogs are held in much higher esteem than in most other parts of the world; and in China and Japan at that time the idea of a celebrity dog was quite unimaginable. When the *Victoria* docked in Yokohama, Japan, and Owney walked down the gangplank, the Japanese customs inspectors were astounded. Here was an ordinary-looking little dog wearing a gem-studded gold collar, owning a lifetime pass on the great American railroad system, occupying his own stateroom on the ship and eating in the officers' mess. Either the American sailors were all crazy or this was some dog!

Whatever the case might be, the officials had to report it to the Emperor; and when that august personage heard the story, he immediately directed that the animal be brought before him. And so it was that Owney, clad in his famous collar and a specially designed jacket, went to pay his respects to the Emperor of Japan. He was an immediate hit. The Sun God was so impressed with the dog's status and behavior that he awarded him a gold medal and directed that he be made an honorary Japanese citizen.

And if the Japanese had done this, could their old rivals the Chinese do less? Not likely, so when the *Victoria* steamed into Shanghai a message from the ruler of the Ch'ing Dynasty was waiting. It was addressed to Owney. So there was another state reception, another medal (more magnificent than the last) and another new citizenship.

But, alas, the ship had reached its final destination and would now be returning to the United States. Would this be the end of Owney's travels? No, not by a long sight. By now every American living in the Orient knew of the dog, and many felt duty bound to assist him in his journey. Wherever the U.S. mails went Owney should be able to go. So when the *Victoria* sailed home from Shanghai, the dog went west traveling again by rail, this time in the keeping of an American consular official going to India on assignment.

And India almost proved the traveler's downfall. He was fascinated by the sights, smells and sounds of ancient Bombay, and he slipped out one night to explore. It was a near fatal mistake. Thieves spotted the dog and, coveting both his valuable collar and his potential as a tasty meal, spirited him away to the slum quarter. Fortunately, the culprits were observed, and police were soon sent in pursuit. They arrived not a moment too soon, for when the officers broke down the thieves' door they found a pot of water already boiling on the fire! But Owney was saved and his collar restored.

Throughout 1896 and 1897 the traveler continued his journey through the Near East and Europe. Sometimes he was accompanied by a diplomat, sometimes by a soldier, a missionary or a businessman; but wherever he went there was someone to care for him and an official postal cancellation to be added to those on his collar.

Occasionally Owney would slip into and out of a country without notice, but in most cases he and his temporary master's arrival at a border check post would lead to an invitation for an audience with government officials and the seemingly inevitable medals and honors. By now, the former had accumulated to such an extent that they could not be worn even on brief state occasions. They had to be carried in a special box passed on from one to another of the dog's guardians.

Back in Albany, George and the other postmen had only the vaguest idea of their pet's whereabouts. They had heard of his visit to Alaska, knew he had sailed to the Orient and had basked in reflected glory when he received medals in Japan and China. After that, it was all pretty uncertain. At one point they learned he was in Tibet. Then there was a report about his being knighted by some Near Eastern sheik. After that, silence.

George worried some at first, but then he thought of that trip to Buffalo. Owney could take care of himself wherever he was. No doubt they would hear from him again in time. The old postman was so right!

It was only a few weeks before the papers carried the news—shocking news. At a formal state reception, Owney had bitten the Emperor of Austria-Hungary on the ankle, apparently because the monarch had failed to give him the medal which he had come to expect at such occasions. The dog had barely escaped from the country with his life, and only then by being spirited across the border in a sack of mail, naturally.

Well, that was enough for George. He was convinced that Owney had had enough of traveling and that the dog had better come home while he was all in one piece. So George contacted the Postmaster General's office and asked officials there to see if they could get the dog back to the United States.

It wasn't hard to find Owney now. The papers in western Europe were full of his exploits. The bite that had made him an outcast in Austria had made him a hero in France, and he was received in Paris as a national hero. The Assembly voted him into membership, and the President awarded him honors due to a head of state. It is true, of course, that when presenting Owney with the coveted Legion of Honor, the President did wear rather high leather boots. But in any case all went very well; and were it not for George, the dog might have settled down in France to a life of ease.

But George Bircher was a persistent man, and he wanted his dog back. Moreover, now that Owney was an international celebrity many Americans also wanted to see him. So, it wasn't too long before the American Ambassador in Paris got a message directing him to make arrangements for Owney's return to the United States. However, about this time another invitation arrived. Queen Victoria wanted to see Owney and to award him a knighthood (the English didn't much like the Austro-Hungarians either). As such a great honor could not be ignored, it was arranged that the dog would be shipped home by way of London.

The reception in England was nearly as tumultuous as that in France had been, and neither compared to what awaited Owney when he finally arrived back in the United States. When his ship docked at San Francisco, thousands of people jammed the pier; and the dog, resplendent in his collar and medals, was given a parade through the city.

After a few days on the West Coast Owney headed back to Albany traveling in his own special parlor car and being feted along the way at receptions in the principal cities. He had become a national hero.

It was several weeks before Owney was finally returned to the old post office building in Albany, and George Bircher found that he scarcely recognized his pet. He had grown so fat and lazy that he hardly moved at all, and he was so covered with ribbons and medals that he looked like a walking jewelry store. And the dog's personality had also changed. He would have nothing at all to do with other dogs and, with the exception of George, showed little interest in people except at mealtimes. Owney had become a snob.

George tried to get him back into the old routine again. He even encouraged Owney to take a few short rides on the local line, but the dog seemed bored with it all. He was now over nine years old, and he had seen everything. He was quite content to just sit around the office looking at his medals, which were prominently displayed in a secure place near the big iron safe.

Nearly a year had passed thus when one night a new guard recently assigned to the post office thought that he heard a noise in the darkened mail room. Suddenly a shadow moved along the wall. The panicked guard thrust his rifle through the half-opened door and pulled the trigger. Something fell to the floor. When the employee turned on the lights, he discovered that he had killed Owney. The dog had just gone in to look at his medals.

And so Owney died, but even in death fame would not desert him. His body was preserved and taken, along with his two hundred medals, to the Postal Museum at Washington, D.C., where they remained until being transferred to the Smithsonian in 1937.

The Bear and
His Brother

Serge was only a half mile from the village when he heard the troops. They must be drunk, he thought, for they were singing loudly and very much off key. The boy looked around for some place to hide. No one wanted to be on the same road with Czarist recruits, least of all when they had been drinking. But the bare dirt path was steep and narrow, and it wound between two high banks. There was no place to hide and no way to go but back. Serge shifted the heavy load of firewood which was bound to his shoulders and turned away.

The men were very near now, just around the next bend, and the lad tried to hurry. But the track was slippery from recent rains. He stumbled, and then suddenly he fell. Head over heels, Serge tumbled right back into the path of the oncoming soldiers!

"What's this?" cried their leader, a huge dirty-faced brute. "The whole forest is rolling down the road. I'll have none of that. Up, boy, and out of our way." With that he seized Serge and dragged him to his feet.

"Wait," cried another soldier, more unkempt-looking than the first, "it's nearly noon and we haven't beaten a single peasant today. Let's start with this one."

"Well said, Nikolai," responded the first, and they both

began pummeling Serge. The child howled with pain and cried aloud for help, but none came, for the Russian peasants greatly feared the ruthless troops.

But then suddenly a great roar echoed through the valley. The startled soldiers stopped striking Serge and looked about them with misgiving. They could hear a terrible growling and a sound like some great beast smashing his way through the dense forest. And indeed it was a great beast, for above them on the hillside a large bear suddenly appeared. For a moment the animal looked down at the men and the boy, then he started rapidly down.

The soldiers turned to flee. They did not get far. Snarling and snapping, the bear fell upon them like a thunderbolt. The first man he seized was tossed down a steep hillside. The second was pushed topsy-turvy into a deep mud puddle. Neither would forget that day for a long time. Then, his work done, the bear ambled slowly up to Serge with almost a smile playing across his furry face. It was Kola, the boy's pet.

Kola the bear was born just prior to the First World War in the rugged hills not far from Tiflis in what is now the Georgian Soviet Socialist Republic. Even then there were few bears left in that area. The constant cutting of trees for fuel and for building materials left little room for animals; and, worse yet, hunters constantly roamed the forests. It was because of them, in fact, that Kola became acquainted with Serge.

In later years Kola remembered little of his first days. He never forgot, however, that terrible morning when he awoke coughing and gagging in the deep cave where he lived with his mother. Hunters had found their hideaway and had set a fire to drive them out.

As the smoke grew thicker, the mother bear rose from her bed, leaving the frightened cub behind. She knew well the danger of fire, and she could smell an even greater threat—man. The she-bear burst out of the cave like a shot from a gun, scattering the burning embers which barred its entrance. She threw herself on the startled men with a wrath born of desperation. The first fell before her great claws never to rise again. She had the second down and would have finished him as well, but the third came up behind and put a bullet through her head. Thus the great bear died, and Kola became an orphan.

And indeed his life too might have been a short one had it not been for Serge's uncle, Grisham, who was one of those who came to the forest to bear away the body of the dead hunter. Many marveled at the size of the fallen bear, but only he among them noticed that she had been nursing. A nursing bear, of course, must have a cub; so, in search of such a one, Grisham crawled deep into the cave. There he found what he had sought. Huddled in the farthest corner and mewing piteously was Kola. He was hungry and alone, and he had not yet learned to fear men. When Grisham reached for him, he came willingly into his arms, and he clung gratefully to the man's heavy fur coat, seeking warmth and nourishment.

Thus it was that Kola was brought to Serge's home, for the Uncle had no room, and besides he well knew who would care most for the young waif. And right he was, for Kola was accepted not as a pet but as a member of the family. Serge, as it happened, had neither brother nor sister, and his home was isolated from the rest of the village. The boy had longed for a companion, someone to play with and to confide in. Kola became that one. The bear slept at the foot of Serge's bed, ate with him at the table and accompanied him to school.

And he shared the boy's life in other ways as well. Children have a gift for communicating with animals, not, of course, in a literal sense but on an emotional level. Serge was a dreamer and a talker, but prior to Kola's arrrival he had had no one who was willing to listen. His parents were too busy, other children too far away. Now he would sit for hours in the woods or fields telling Kola of his hopes and aspirations. A poor boy, he dreamed of riches and of travel, of going to St. Petersburg, to Moscow, of seeing the Czar, of having a fine house and a good business. All this he told to his friend, and the bear listened. True, he did not answer, and it is not likely that he understood. But, he was there. A bond was formed between man and animal that would endure for a lifetime.

Now, of course, this was not all of Kola's life. As he grew older, the bear was taught many of the traditional skills for which his kind are noted: to shake hands, to dance, to wrestle and to balance a ball on his nose. Yet, for the most part, he spent his time with the boy, and he was raised as the boy was raised, learning to carry firewood, to drag stone from the fields and wood to the mill.

Indeed, as his size increased, the bear became a source of some concern to those who were Serge's neighbors. He had been taught never to bite or frighten people; but still a watchdog of such great strength made visitors uncomfortable.

It was most fortunate, therefore, that the incident with the soldiers occurred when it did. The peasants of the Tiflis region had long hated and feared the raw recruits who came each summer to train in their fields and forests. The Czar's men were undisciplined brutes who stole what they could and constantly abused their unwilling hosts. It was no surprise then that once the story of Kola's exploits had reached the ears of his neighbors they saw him in a very different light. He was no longer a monster. He was now a protector. For the soldiers avoided the village as though it were an armed camp. They never knew when the dreaded bear might appear.

Kola now became an honored citizen. When he walked through the village alone or with Serge, men and women gave him admiring glances or even came up to shake his hand. Children were bolder. They rode on the bear's back or threw balls for him to catch. And, of course, he had all he could eat and more. He was, in short, the toast of the town.

Still, there were those who did not trust or like the bear or who perhaps could not really believe that such an animal could not be dangerous. So great was Kola's prestige within the community that such people could not speak against him openly, but when the chance appeared they would play tricks upon him or steal his food. Kola saw this and it angered him, but he never thought to injure his tormentors. He did, however, have other ways of dealing with them.

There was, for example, the town carpenter, a mean man who delighted in tormenting Kola by spoiling his food or stealing his ball when Serge was not around. The bear endured this abuse for a while, then he decided to take his revenge. He waited until the workman's back was turned, then snatched his packet of nails and dumped them into a pail of dirty water. While the annoyed carpenter looked everywhere for the missing nails, the bear also took his hammer and quietly sat down upon it. The man's day was ruined. For hours he looked for the vanished tools while his fellow townsmen hooted in amusement (he was not a popular fellow) and the bear sat calmly by watching him. Only when the great animal rose and ambled off did the carpenter realize that he had been tricked. After that he treated Kola with more respect.

And so for nearly six years Kola and Serge lived in the little village. The boy grew to young manhood and the bear to his full size and power. Often the animal would go off into the forest for days to hunt and to be with his own kind. However, he always returned to his home and his master.

But good things must so often come to an end, and so it was with friendship of bear and boy. One day a government messenger came to the village. The news he brought was grim. War had broken out far away in the west, and Russia was assailed by her ancient enemy, Germany. All the able-bodied young men of the region must go to defend their homeland. Serge had never liked soldiers, and he was sure that he would not like war, yet he knew he must go. But what was he to do with his bear? Uncle Grisham was away, and there was no one else he could trust with his friend.

Then Serge remembered. Two years before a small circus had come to the village. Its owner, a kindly man named Nikita, had owned a bear, and Serge had been greatly impressed with the love and respect that he had shown for his beast. Moreover, Nikita had wanted to buy Kola and had told the boy to come to him if he ever needed a home for his pet.

Two days later Serge and Kola set out on foot for Tiflis. It was nearly a day's walk, and dusk was settling on the country-side when they reached the great city. The young man did not know where to find the circus owner, but he knew where to look. Trained bears were frequently displayed in taverns and hotels; so, one after another, he visited these asking after a certain bear and its master. Late in the evening he found a barkeeper who remembered a man who trained bears. He sounded like Nikita, and he lived in a building just a few blocks away. Eagerly, Serge and Kola sought out the house. They knocked at the door and the man they sought opened it. He was delighted to see his old friends and even more delighted to learn that Kola was to stay with him. Nikita's own bear had just died, and a new one would be a welcome addition to the little circus.

And so Serge and Kola parted. The boy put on a uniform and went away to fight on the western front. The bear became a performer traveling with his new master through the tiny towns of southern Georgia. Two years passed.

It was in the spring of 1916 that Serge returned to Tiflis. For months he had served the Czar on the far borders of the Empire. He had been hungry and cold and had seen his comrades die like flies all about him, but he had survived; and now he was going home on a well-earned leave. He longed to see his family and friends, but most of all he wished to see Kola.

From the train station Serge went straight to Nikita's house. But his knock at the door drew no response; and, worse yet, inquiries among the neighbors brought the sad report that the circus was no more. Its owner too had been taken into the army. He had been gone for nearly a year, and no one knew what had happened to the bear. One day, just before he was to leave for the front, Nikita had taken Kola away. That was all that anyone knew.

Serge spent most of his precious leave looking for his old friend. He visited all the towns in the vicinity of Tiflis and wandered the streets of the city itself asking everyone he met if they had seen his bear. No one had. In the end, the young man even took to walking in the neighboring woods calling for Kola. There was no response.

At last, worn out from his search and with all hope gone, the young soldier went back to his village. There he chanced to meet his Uncle Grisham, who had also just returned after a long time away. The family was so delighted to have both of them back at once that they decided upon a celebration. Not far from Tiflis there was a little country inn nestled in a pine woods. It was there that the family decided to go.

It was a grand feast. The table overflowed with all sorts of good food, and many of Serge's friends from the village came to pay their respects to the returning hero. A great number of toasts were drunk, songs sung and fine speeches made, but the guest of honor had great difficulty keeping his mind on the festivities. Ever and again his thoughts would stray to Kola. Would he ever see him again? Tomorrow he must return to the army, and he had failed in his quest.

As the clock struck twelve, Serge rose, as was the custom, to make the final toast. He thanked all who had come and spoke aloud of his love for his lost friend. Then, more as a gesture than in hope of response, he once more called Kola's name. But this time there was an answer.

From deep within the building there came an answering roar. A great din was heard in the kitchen, a smashing of glass and a clanging of pots. Then suddenly the door to the dining room burst open and a great form towered over the diners. From one leg dangled a stake and chain. His arms were outstretched in greeting. It was Kola!

The boy and the bear fell into each other's arms in joy while the other guests cheered and clapped each other on the back. They had never witnessed such a miracle before. More wine was brought and the celebration was prolonged far into the night. There were now three guests of honor.

And, of course, the whole story came out. The innkeeper was Nikita's brother. When the circus owner learned that he had to go away to war, he brought Kola to the country, feeling that the animal would be safest there. But now Nikita would never return. He had fallen on a faraway battlefield, and though his brother had heard of Serge he did not know where he was or when he would return from the war. Therefore, respecting his brother's wishes, the innkeeper had fed and cared for the bear. But he really didn't like animals, particularly such large ones; and he had kept Kola locked for months in a dark outbuilding. It was from there that the bear had heard his master's last hopeless call; and with love lending strength to his limbs, he had torn up the stake to which he was bound and made his way to the dining room.

So now Serge had a decision to make. Clearly Kola could not stay at the inn. Nikita's brother was a good man, but he could never overcome his fear of the great bear. Nor could Kola stand to be chained for months, perhaps years, in a cold, dark building while he awaited his master's return. And worse, thought Serge, what if he did not return? War was terrible and fate uncertain. Look at poor Nikita. What if he too were to die in battle? Kola would be doomed to a life of imprisonment. Something clearly had to be done, and the young soldier knew what it was.

The moon was just rising over the thick pine woods when the boy and the bear walked slowly up the hill from the inn. It was late and all was quiet. Far below, the lights of the buildings sparkled against the dark fields. They were leaving the world of people.

They entered the deep forest. Kola's ears pricked up and he rumbled deep in his throat, a rumble of pleasure not anger. His nose twitched with anticipation. The bear was surrounded by the sights and smells of his youth. He was at home. Serge sensed the change and knew it was right. This was where the bear should be, where he would have a chance of survival. True, the animal had lived his life primarily in captivity, but his frequent sojourns in the deep woods had prepared him against this day. Better the uncertain chances of a natural existence then the certain misery of an unnatural one.

Serge once more, for the final time, took the bear's huge paw in his. Kola nuzzled the young man's curly hair. It was a long loving handshake and a final parting. Then, without a word, Serge turned and headed back down into the valley. The bear watched him go, but he did not follow.

Special Privileges

The crowd in the Colosseum rose as one man, and ten thousand voices were raised in a single cry: "Incitatus! Incitatus! On! On!" Below them on the dusty track the great dappled gelding was making his move for the lead. For more than half the race his driver had been content to stay behind the leaders, but now he swung his terrible leather whip across the team of three straining horses and urged them forward. The black and the bay faltered momentarily, but Incitatus took the bit in his foam-flecked teeth and bulled ahead. Not without reason was he considered the finest lead horse in all of Italy. He loved to race, and he hated to lose.

For Incitatus it had always been thus. Born in northern Italy, in the foothills of the Alps, he had been regarded almost from birth as an exceptional animal. He was large as a foal and grew more rapidly than his peers, so that even as a yearling he was nearly as large as a full-grown horse. Now at four he was fully seventeen hands high and as powerfully muscled as a dray horse.

Moreover, where most horses had to be trained to race, Incitatus seemed born to it; and at an early age he had broken out of his stall to join a group of chariot steeds training on a nearby track. The speed the colt showed that day convinced his handlers that he should be trained as a lead horse, and after that it was easy. The gelding swept through the provincial tracks like a rising storm, and within a year he was in Rome competing at the great Colosseum. It was there that the eyes of royalty fell upon him.

High in the stands, in the place of honor, the Emperor of all the Romans rose to his feet—Caligula, the crazy, the hated and the feared. The Emperor's eyes rolled in his head with excitement, his purple robes were damp with sweat. All morning he had waited for this race, for this moment, for this horse! He loved Incitatus with a passion unnatural to a man who seemed to live only for hate and destruction, and now his favorite was once more coming to the fore. Caligula gripped the edge of his gold-encrusted royal box and watched the drama unfolding below.

There was a half mile to go, twice more around the rutted track, and Incitatus's chariot trailed by four lengths. But the great horse was going flat out now, almost dragging his two harness mates off the ground as he thundered after the leaders. At the first turn he surged past the Dalmatian team, the wheels of the two chariots temporarily locking while the drivers beat each other viciously with their quirts. The Emperor shouted with glee as his favorite's driver slashed his opponent across the eyes, causing the Dalmatian chariot to careen wildly into a wall.

But there were still the upstart horses from Mediolanum. Grimly the provincial driver clung to the lead, always conscious of the gelding's approaching hoofbeats but even more conscious of something else. Like all the other drivers, he knew that Incitatus's team had been beaten but once before. On that momentous occasion the Emperor had called the winning driver to his suite to be "suitably rewarded." That driver had not been seen again. Was winning really all that important?

And so it was that when the two chariots, neck and neck at last, rolled down the final stretch that led to the finish line, knowledgeable horsemen might have noted that the driver from Mediolanum was pulling back on the reins . . . just a little, just enough. If there were those who noticed, none said, for they too valued their lives. And, of course, Incitatus won with a rush, and the crowd went predictably wild. Caligula, beside himself with joy, threw handfuls of gold coins to the people below, and the drivers of the losing chariots smiled sadly to themselves at the thought that they would at least live to race again.

That evening something quite unexpected happened. Incitatus's handlers were startled to hear that their steed was not to be taken out to the country as was the usual custom between races. He was to remain in Rome by Imperial order. He was, in fact, to be taken to the palace.

All afternoon, preparations for a feast had been taking place in the palace. Caligula loved banquets, particularly since he knew that so many of his guests attended out of fear rather than affection. But he particularly looked forward to this occasion, for tonight he intended to realize his dream. He knew that he loved Incitatus as he had loved no other creature. The beast's nobility and will to win were overwhelming. It was not enough for him to visit him in the stables, to heap awards upon his drivers and praise upon his handlers. He must have his favorite with him always. Already his messengers were at the stables announcing the edict. Henceforth, Incitatus, royal steed, would be housed in a way befitting his rank and character. He would live with the Emperor of Rome!

Incitatus's owners were stunned. They well knew the Emperor's fondness for their beast; and indeed they had profited by it more than once, since they well understood the reluctance of other drivers to urge their horses past a royal favorite. But now to lose the animal when there was still so much money to be made! Of course, there was the vague promise of return, but all men knew better. Anything or anyone who fell into Caligula's hands never returned, at least not in its original condition. And there was no point in protesting. A long unhappy life was pref-

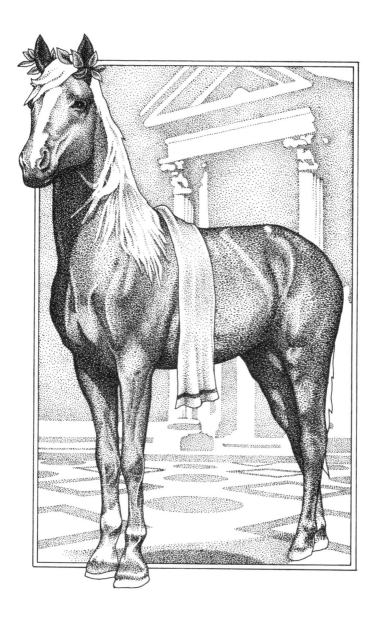

erable to a short unhappy one. Their faces suffused with false smiles, the owners gave up their horse and watched as Incitatus was led away toward the royal dwellings.

A short time later the guests gathered before the great banquet table. Their togas were spotless, their golden jewelry abundant; but their faces were somber. What madness would Caligula devise this time? Who would be humiliated? Who would be convicted? Who would just disappear? At the Emperor's banquet the guests provided the entertainment, and they hated it. But none dared to refuse an invitation. To do so would be considered treason, and the penalty for that was well known.

They glanced at the royal dais. Tonight it was larger than usual. Was Caligula having special guests or did he plan to execute someone during the meal? The macabre joke went its rounds, but few laughed. They had seen too much madness during this Emperor's reign to laugh easily.

At exactly the hour appointed, the curtains on the dais rose and then the guests knew. Seated at the right, his stiff black hair crowned with a golden diadem, was Caligula. To his left, sitting back on his haunches, a laurel wreath about his brow, was Incitatus. Purple robes of state hung about his shoulders, and golden dishes were before him on the table. The guest of honor was a horse!

Caligula beamed down at those assembled before him, then turned to his equine companion. He ran his hands lovingly over Incitatus's long neck and, drawing the horse's head toward him, he planted a kiss on his cheek. However this might have seemed to others, the affection was genuine. Caligula loved this steed more than anyone or anything alive. Indeed, the horse was the only thing he cared for other than power and cruelty.

For months he had worshiped the beast from afar. Now he had him at his side. The Emperor murmured softly, his head buried in the horse's mane, then turned to those seated below him. "This is Incitatus, my closest friend and honored guest. It is my wish that you will welcome him as befits his rank."

The crowd seethed with ill-concealed rage. Stealing and kill-ing were one thing—after all, so many emperors had indulged in those vices that they had become almost a mark of royalty—but to insult the leading citizens of Rome by asking them to pay their respects to a horse, that was unspeakable. And yet they had no choice. The room was ringed with soldiers, and behind the Emperor's smile there was a steely madness. He would tol-erate no dissent. Slowly, reluctantly, the nobles rose; one by one they bowed before the horse.

The rest of the evening passed without incident. Indeed, the Emperor paid little attention to his guests (which certainly suited them), focusing all his concern on the horse.

It is doubtful that this attention meant much to Incitatus. The horse was extremely uneasy. He was frightened by the bright lights, the sounds and the horrible smell of cooking meat. His position was extremely uncomfortable, and he was prevented from shifting it by an ingenious tether rigged beneath the table. For him, as for the guests, the evening passed much too slowly.

Nor was Caligula interested in prolonging the festivities. Having amused himself at his guests' expense, he had no further need for them at the moment; and besides he had something else to do. He wanted to show Incitatus his new stall.

And so, quite abruptly, the banquet was terminated and the visitors ushered out. The horse was released and led down into the Emperor's private quarters. There a stable had been pre-pared such as no horse had ever occupied. Its walls were of marble, and upon them hung fine paintings. The manger was carved ivory; and instead of from a bucket, Incitatus was to drink from a golden bowl!

A group of specially trained slaves awaited the horse's com-ing. Some were musicians assigned to play tunes to calm the savage beast, others were stable hands responsible for grooming him each day, a task which included gilding Incitatus's hoofs and weaving dozens of colored ribbons into his mane. Never had a horse been so pampered!

His arm encircling the horse's neck, Caligula led his favorite into his new quarters. "There, my lovely, there it is and all for you," he purred. "No other beast has ever been so honored, but none other have I loved or trusted as I do you. I live my life surrounded by enemies, by those who would steal all that I have and kill me as well if they dared. Only you can I depend upon, and to you I will give all." His heart almost bursting with joy, the Emperor of all the Romans released the horse to his minions' care.

One should not, however, assume that Incitatus was pleased with all this attention. He was not. For him, life consisted of racing and the familiar smells and sounds of the open fields, the race course and the stables. He hated the hard marble floors of his new home, the total lack of equine companionship and the constant fussing of his attendants. As the weeks passed, the horse grew more morose. He missed racing desperately, and he loathed the banquets. Each time he was required to attend he made it more difficult for those who were assigned to escort him him to the banquet hall and to tether him at the table. He was reaching the breaking point.

The Emperor's dinner guests were approaching a similar crisis. Each week, in fact several times each week, they were forced to eat dinner with a horse. Their friends, those fortunate enough to be of such low estate as to not rate invitations, laughed at them. On the streets and in the forum, slaves and citizens pointed and laughed behind their hands. Everyone in Rome knew of the banquets and the "guest of honor," and each man wished nothing more for his worst enemy than an invitation to dine at the royal table!

It was at this point that Caligula made a serious mistake. Though seemingly oblivious to his guests' discomfort, he knew well what they were experiencing, and it delighted him. But he was growing weary of the repetitive dinners. Something more must be done to humiliate the nobles.

And so it was that when the unfortunates next arrived, they

found that a slight change had been made in the seating arrangements. Incitatus was no longer in his usual place on the dais. He had seemingly been demoted. He was, in fact, now seated among them clad in the same white silk napkin and jeweled collar which they affected.

Those guests closest to the animal squirmed with discomfort and tried to move as far away from him as possible, while their more fortunate companions looked on with horror. What would happen next? They did not wait long to find out.

The trumpets blew. The slaves brought in the first course. It consisted of elaborately stuffed and baked chicken. As the servants moved slowly down the long table serving each guest with an individually prepared bird, the nobles watched with a growing sense of apprehension. Incitatus had never been fed at the banquets. Why was he now wearing a bib? Could it be that the beast was to be offered the very food that they were expected to dine upon?

And, yes, that was Caligula's intention. When the servers reached the horse, they did not hesitate, even for an instant. Acting as though he were but another citizen, they thrust a large fowl onto his plate and set it before him. The animal smelled the horrible odor of cooked flesh. His eyes rolled with terror. He did not do what the Emperor had hoped he would, though it is difficult to imagine how even Caligula could have expected him to really eat meat. What he did was something quite different.

Gathering himself with a mighty and convulsive effort, Incitatus reared back from the table, shattering his bonds and bringing the heavily laden board down with a great crash. Then, free of restraint, he charged straight through the terrified throng, knocking people left and right as he bolted for the door. Once through that, he did not stop until he had reached the comparative safety of his stall.

It was a chastened group of nobles who filed slowly from the dining room that memorable night. That horse had shown them all something of dignity. If he, a mere animal, could not tolerate the indignity heaped upon him by the tyrant, how could they, the leading citizens of Rome, suffer it in silence?

Gradually the men and women drew together, at first just trusted friends, then small groups and, finally, in a great throng where, personal animosities forgotten for the moment, they resolved to stand together. No one or two could refuse the hated invitations. Punishment for that would come swiftly. But what if all refused? Could Caligula kill them all at once? No, he could not. With their servants and dependents they numbered many thousands, including high-ranking officers in the army. They realized for the first time a growing sense of power. Together they could be more powerful than the Emperor.

And so it came to pass that when Caligula held his next banquet, no one came, not even Incitatus; for the horse had refused to leave his stall, and two slaves were now nursing broken bones acquired in trying to change his mind. The Emperor sat alone on his high dais looking out over a vast empty hall. Not a single noble had arrived.

Caligula pounded his golden wine cup on the marble table. His face turned red with rage. They had humiliated him. What to do? A dozen mad plots surged through his addled brain. He would poison them all. He would enslave their families, burn their estates. No, none of that would work, not with such a large group. Even he could not defeat the nobles as long as they stood together. He would have to think of something else, something that would pull apart this dangerous union.

The high-ranking citizens naturally awaited the tyrant's next move with considerable apprehension. The first few days after the disastrous banquet had passed without incident, and they saw that they had been right as far as mass retaliation was concerned. Caligula did not intend to murder them all, at least not yet. They had no doubt, though, that he planned some terrible revenge. Just what it would be they could not guess.

When it came, the counterstroke was brilliant in its cruelty. The Emperor, a week or so after the dinner, announced to the

Senate that he had determined to share power with a consul, a position currently vacant, but one of such exalted stature that it had been held by, among others, Julius Caesar.

Who would the new leader be? No one could guess; but immediately the highest-ranking nobles, forgetting their hatred of Caligula, swarmed around him seeking the post. The old resolve to stand together against tyranny began to come apart in the face of the burning desire to share power. The rich began to scheme against each other. This was just what the wily demagogue had hoped for.

The tyrant had victory nearly within his grasp. He could toy with the greedy nobles, playing one off against the other, until they were thoroughly divided, then crush them all piecemeal. It should have worked well; but, of course, Caligula was mad. He couldn't resist adding one further insult to the pot, and that was the straw that broke the camel's ack.

Not waiting for the coalition of nobles to completely disintegrate, he precipitously went before the Senate once more. This time he announced that his choice was made. The assembeld lawmakers waited breathlessly. Who would it be?

The Emperor smiled a wolfish smile. "I have chosen," he said, "that one who is closest to me, most trustworthy and most fit to represent you all. I have chosen Incitatus. If you will not dine with him, you will be ruled by him."

The decision fell like a thunderclap. They had never thought that even Caligula would go so far; and he, for his part, had misjudged the patience of his subjects. As he left the Senate that day, he stood, though he did not know it, alone against all of Rome.

Within hours the old union had been re-established and the decision made. The tyrant must die. After that it was absurdly easy. Even the Emperor's bodyguard had turned against him; and when they were approached, two soldiers readily agreed to do the deed. The next time Caligula went to visit Incitatus, he was welcomed not by his chosen consul but by assassins. No one came to his aid as the tyrant fell beneath a flurry of blows.

For his part, Incitatus was pleased with the result. He soon found himself in the country once more, free to run and feed. He could never race again, for it would have raised too many unpleasant memories, but he was assured a long and peaceful life. The nobles did not after all hold grudges against a horse whom many saw as the spark of their liberation.

A Mother's Choice

The hillside had been burned not so long ago, and as the she-fox crossed the open area her paws left tiny depressions in the gray dust stubble. She moved slowly and heavily, for her time to deliver was near. The cubs moved in her belly like a rising storm. She would have to get to the den soon.

The vixen was almost halfway across the burned-over area when she saw the hunters. There were two of them, and they had a dog, a big cur who moved back and forth across the path, his shaggy head sweeping the air for scent. The fox froze. She was too far from the trees to run for it. A bullet would surely find her on the way. She looked about. Two gray boulders rose out of the fire-blackened soil. There was no other cover. The fox had an idea. She lay down curling her tail across her face.

Arnold Hicken scanned the burned hillside for some sign of life—preferably fox life. He was sick of foxes. They were driving him to distraction with their nightly raids on the hen coops. For over a month now he had lost two or three chickens each evening, despite barred doors and a high wire fence. Neither skunks nor raccoons could get into henhouses protected that way. It could only mean one thing. A fox, or perhaps two foxes, had taken up residence in the neighborhood.

The dog moved uncertainly, his big nose sucking in the wind currents. The breeze had for a moment shifted, blowing downhill from where the vixen lay. A tantalizing odor had come to the mongrel, but only for a moment. The wind was now blowing again uphill, from the hunters to the fox. The scent was gone. The dog swept back and forth across the lower hillside, his head bobbing as he hunted for the elusive scent.

"Do you think he has something, Bob?" Hicken asked, turning to his companion. "He acts like he's onto a trail."

"Not likely," responded Bob Ambruster. "He's not tracking. Something interesting in the wind, a rabbit maybe, but not a fox. You wouldn't catch them in the open this time of day. Besides, where would it be? There's nothing on this hillside but rocks and burnt grass."

Arnold ran his eyes slowly across the face of the hill. His friend was right. Nothing up there, just those three rocks and some burnt pasture. The dog too had calmed down and had resumed his usual frisking about before the hunters. Whatever had disturbed him had passed.

The hunters moved on across the meadow and passed slowly out of sight beneath the trees of an adjoining wood. The vixen watched them go, her shrewd black eyes peering from beneath the gray tail. When they were gone she rose. There were now only two boulders on the dreary hill.

Had Hicken known how close his quarry had been he would have been upset; but it would have proven even more upsetting had he realized that the fox was frequently even closer. She, in fact, lived next door! The vixen had chosen her home for convenience. Working only at night, she had dug a burrow on the small island which lay in the river just a few hundred feet from Hicken's farmhouse. There she had easy access to the food with which she planned to feed her offspring as well as an almost foolproof escape route, for the water masked her goings and comings.

And, of course, the burrow itself was cunningly concealed.

Thick brambles covered the entire island, and through these the fox had tunneled a small passage barely a foot in diameter. This led to the mouth of the den, which itself was hidden under a hollow cottonwood tree. Any pursuer would have to chop down the tree in order to reach the tunnel which led to the underground burrow. It was all very clever but hardly unusual for a fox.

That night the foxes were born, all four of them. Through the long hours of darkness the mother nursed and cared for her offspring, and when she was through it was daylight. She was very hungry, but it was no time to visit the poultry house. The vixen would have to look elsewhere. She rose and stole from the burrow. The tiny foxes, all in a huddle, slept soundly.

Hicken was puzzled. He had fully expected to find chickens missing this morning, yet there was no sign of the usual nocturnal visit. Had the fox left? Had someone else killed it? No matter, at least he had suffered no loss that night; and perhaps his good fortune would continue. This day at least he would go to the fields to work, not to hunt.

Meanwhile, the object of the farmer's concern was herself on the hunt. Moving swiftly through the beech forest, the vixen soon reached an area of nut-bearing trees. Then she began to watch the treetops. She soon spotted what she was seeking. High in the boughs sat a red squirrel. The fox moved slowly into his view; then suddenly she reared into the air, whirled about and fell to the ground. She did not move again.

For a long time the squirrel watched the still form of the vixen. What was she doing there in his forest and what had happened to her? The small animal well knew the danger of foxes, but his curiosity was thoroughly aroused; and, besides, the great beast didn't look dangerous now. He crept down the tree till he crouched on a branch a dozen feet above the object of his attention, then he began to chatter. The fox didn't seem to mind the scolding. Perhaps she didn't hear it. Now the squirrel was really annoyed, but he had another idea. In a moment he was gone. In a moment he was back bearing several large acorns. These he dropped on the vixen's back. No result.

Now the squirrel was beginning to believe that there was really something wrong with the fox. Prudence warned him to stay away, but he just couldn't stand to leave there without finding out what had happened. The squirrel came cautiously down the tree trunk, poised to flee at the slightest sign of life. The fox lay like a stone.

The squirrel reached the ground. Step by step, he crossed the open area that lay between him and the fox. At last he stood at her head. An eye opened. The vixen seemed to smile. On his first leap the squirrel covered half the distance to the tree. He did not make a second leap. The fox fell on him like a gray thunderbolt. Now she too would eat.

It was on the following night that the farmer learned his luck had not changed. Just before dawn he heard his dog barking down at the chicken coops. He was on his feet in an instant, and, pausing only for a pair of pants and a gun, he headed for the door.

Halfway to the coops he could see that he was too late. The fox had made her selection and even now was heading for home. By the light of the single bulb hanging over the shed door he could see the vixen as she leaped the high fence. A full-grown hen was dangling from her jaws. Hicken got off a snap shot, but the range was long and the light poor. The fox didn't pause to give him a second shot.

But the dog was after her in a minute, and when the farmer reached the riverbank he found his faithful beast running up and down the bank. The scent was lost in the water, and there was no sign of the fox on the far side. How could she have gotten across so quickly? Hicken looked hard at the little island. Nothing moved there, but he resolved to look the place over soon. It wasn't really big enough to shelter a fox, but one could never be sure.

Meanwhile, the vixen was resting comfortably in her den surrounded by her family. In the morning she would eat the hen. Now she would nurse her babies and contemplate her narrow escape.

Indeed, it seemed that her life was nothing but a succession of escapes and babies. How many litters had she had by now? She could not recall. Each year there had been a male (he had seldom stayed long) and then the little ones. Most had survived, at least to the point where they had suddenly gone off on their own; some had not. Hunters, dogs, disease, all had taken their toll. She had loved and cared equally for all. The vixen did not question her life. She only lived it.

A few days and several chickens later, Arnold Hicken decided that it was time to visit the island. The fact of the fox's sudden disappearance preyed on his mind. How was it possible for her to vanish so quickly unless she was taking refuge there?

The deed soon followed the thought, and late that very afternoon Hicken and his dog beached their rowboat on the narrow shore. The dog immediately began to nose about. He could detect a scent. It was old and uncertain but definitely there. Hicken urged him on, his own conviction growing stronger. They worked their way along the shore, drawing ever nearer to the tiny tunnel that led to the den.

Suddenly there was a sound from the far shore. It was the bark of a fox. There she stood right at the water's edge as though challenging them. The mongrel went wild with fury; leaping into the river, he struck out for the opposite bank. Hicken raised his rifle, but the animal he sought was gone. Not far, though, for the sound of her bark could still be heard, just out of sight in the dense woods. Arnold rowed toward her, the island momentarily forgotten.

The vixen watched them come. It had been fortunate for the

pups that she was out that day. Her only hope to distract the hunters was to draw them after her and away from the burrow. She barked again. The dog was wading ashore now. The fox turned and melted into the undergrowth, moving just rapidly enough to stay ahead of her pursuer.

For two hours pursued and pursuers roamed the beech groves, always drawing farther away from the island. Only when darkness approached did the fox end the game. She knew that now there would be no further opportunity to seek the den. Standing on a high hill, outlined against the setting sun, she gave the farmer a last glimpse, then vanished as mysteriously as she had come.

Arnold Hicken was really a kind man, and it was with the greatest reluctance that he took the next step in his escalating war with the fox. Many of his neighbors employed poisoned baits to keep down farm pests, but the idea had never appealed to Hicken. He had seen too many cats and dogs who had been the accidental victims of such a strategy. On the other hand, his own attempts had all proven fruitless. He had seen the fox. He had pursued her. She had easily escaped. He had no doubt that a similar result would attend his next effort. Poison seemed the only alternative.

And so it was that the vixen on her next excursion to the henhouses was surprised to find that she had been left some seemingly choice offerings. Several chicken heads, a food favored by foxes but shunned by most dogs, were scattered near the fence which enclosed the chicken runs. The fox approached these tidbits with some care. They certainly looked appealing, but their presence was suspicious and their odor more so. She recognized a faint acrid aroma, the same one she had detected about the bodies of woodchucks and skunks which she had come across in her roamings through the neighboring woodlands. Those animals had died without signs of violence, and the vixen had associated their deaths with the strange smell. She certainly would not touch the chicken heads.

The fox continued on her way, over the fence and into the coops. The startled hens fluttered in terror as she sprang in among them. The vixen wasted no time, for she knew that the dog would soon be aroused. A quick snatch of the nearest fowl and she was on her way again. And not a moment too soon. The mongrel was nearly at her heels as she reached the river, but he did not relish the dark water: he remained on the bank as she swam swiftly to the island.

Hicken reached the stream well after his cur, for he had wearied of the hopeless nightly excursions. The chase was always in vain, and this night was no exception. Once more he looked out on black and empty waters. The fox was gone.

When several days had passed and the poisoned baits, no matter how cleverly placed, remained untouched, the farmer reluctantly conceded that they too had failed. He could see only one more thing to do. Since he was now convinced that the fox had a den quite near to the farmhouse, he would search for the burrow. And he would start with the island. He had remembered his dog's reaction that day they had seen the fox. The mongrel had acted like he was picking up a scent on the island. They would go there again.

This time luck ran against the vixen. After only a few minutes' search the dog found the fox run, and he quickly followed it to the hollow cottonwood. When Arnold reached the tree, his faithful beast was baying loudly and scratching wildly at the rotted stump. There could be no doubt about it. They had her now. Leaving the dog on watch, the farmer went back for an axe and a shovel.

When the man returned to the island, he was greeted by the piteous howls of the unhappy dog. Running frantically back and forth between the stump and the shore, the beast described all too vividly what had transpired during his absence. The fox had escaped!

Lying deep in her burrow, she had heard the dreaded barking and had known immediately that she had been discovered. The vixen understood only too well that a deep hole was no protection against man. She must escape, but how—and how could she escape with four cubs? There was but one exit, and that was guarded.

The mother looked at her four offspring. There was a way, but only for her and a single cub. She wasted no time on the decision, but simply reached in among the squirming brood and seized the first one that came to hand. With the cub in her jaws she crawled quietly up the tunnel that led to the stump.

As the fox had anticipated, the dog was trying to dig under the tree roots to reach the tunnel. She waited quietly a few inches from his nose until she judged that he was well into the ground, then she came up with a rush. When the dog raised himself from the hole he was digging, it was only to see the fox vanishing into the bushes along the river. She had jumped completely over him! With a howl of dismay he raced after his quarry, but it was too late. When the mongrel reached the water, the vixen, cub held high before her, was already halfway to the far shore.

The farmer looked at his dog and looked at the water. Was the fox gone again? Was it even worth digging the den out now? For a moment he contemplated just going back home. Then he changed his mind. No, he would dig it up if only to see where his foe had been.

The axe bit readily into the old stump. Within a few minutes it was down and the mouth of the den exposed. Then began the real work. It took nearly two hours to reach the burrow, but when he got there Hicken was not disappointed. There, in the farthest corner of the little cave, were the three cubs. The dog was on them in a moment, his fury a terrible thing to see. The farmer, why he didn't know, reached down and pulled one clear. The rest died unpleasantly.

Arnold looked at the tiny fox, its eyes barely open, its mouth wide in piteous yelps. He didn't know why he had saved it. He certainly didn't like foxes. But, one thing he knew, he wouldn't have it killed now. There had been enough of that. He wrapped the kit in his jacket and rowed away from the island.

The vixen didn't stop running until she was deep in the woods. In the back of her mind there was concern for the other three cubs, but at the moment she thought only of herself and of the tiny thing she carried. She must find shelter. It was only after a lengthy search that she discovered a suitable refuge—an old woodchuck hole, stinking and poorly dug but safe. It took her most of the night to reshape the den to her liking, but when she was through she could be sure that her kit would be safe there. Now she must see what could be salvaged on the island.

The farmer had, in the meantime, returned home. Not knowing what else to do with it, he chained the tiny fox in a small shed not far from the house. Since it was not yet weaned, he left the animal a bowl of milk.

In the morning he discovered something interesting. The container of milk was undisturbed, yet the kit seemed fat and contented. Also, the chain, for several inches near the neck, was worn shiny. There was only one explanation. The vixen had found her cub and had both fed and tried unsuccessfully to rescue it. The farmer was amazed. He had never dreamed that such mother love existed among animals. It was with some regret that he determined to take advantage of it to rid himself at last of his old enemy.

The trap Hicken rigged was a terrible one. An old shotgun was attached to the door of the kit's shed so that when the mother pulled it open to enter she would trigger a load of buckshot that would put an end to her maternal instincts. The device was crude but effective.

The moon was still behind the hills and the night black as a pit when the vixen left her new den. She had determined to make one more effort to free the remaining cub; the fate of the other two she already knew. Moving quickly through the woods and across the river, she soon reached the farm. All was quiet, but her nostrils told her where her offspring was imprisoned, and she made her way there. The door was partially ajar. She moved to open it. However, there was something odd about the door. It seemed to be tied to something. The vixen moved about so that she could get a better view. There were wires on the door, and they led to a gun. She could see its outline against the shed wall. The fox knew guns. She had seen them in action and understood that they could kill, though she did not understand why. Instinctively, she recognized that her way was barred.

For a long time the vixen sat in the darkness outside the shed watching her sleeping pup and trying to decide what to do. She knew now that she could not rescue it. Could she leave it to its fate in the hands of cruel man? No, that she would not do. The fox rose and vanished into the blackness. She was gone but a few minutes. When she returned she was carrying a chicken head, one of the poisoned ones which lay outside the hen coop. Her pup would die, of course; but she would have chosen death over captivity, and she could offer it no less. Leaving the deadly tidbit within reach, the vixen turned away. She had done all she could here. There was still a pup alive in the forest burrow, and she must return to care for it. Whatever else, the family must go on.

Monkey See, Monkey Do

From a distance the scene appears in no way unusual—the rolling hills of the Australian sheep country, gray-green in the noonday sun, and the tiny tractor working its way slowly across the wastes. But as the vehicle draws nearer, one notices something out of place. It's the driver. Somehow he doesn't seem quite right. There is an oddness about the way he hunches over the wheel, the set of his shoulders, the bobbing of his head. In a way, he looks scarcely human; and as the tractor comes into full view, it becomes clear that he is not. The figure at the controls, though he is clad in dungarees and shirt and wears a straw hat, is a baboon!

How this remarkable occurrence, certainly one of the more strange in the annals of men and beasts, came to pass is a fascinating story. It starts, strangely enough, with a fire.

Early in 1955 Lindsay Schmidt, an Australian farmer and sheep rancher, was driving into town for supplies when he noticed several large trucks parked along the roadside. One of the vehicles was afire, and a group of men were attempting simultaneously to put out the flames and to rescue something which appeared to be trapped in the rear of the truck.

It was lonely country thereabouts, and Schmidt, like his

neighbors, was accustomed to lending a hand when needed. He quickly pulled over and prepared to assist the firefighters. Fortunately Lindsay carried a large fire extinguisher in his truck, and this proved to be just what was needed. The flames were confined to the engine, and a judicious application of fire retardant foam soon smothered them. Within moments the crisis was past, and the sheepman was the center of grateful attention.

"Many thanks, matey," remarked a large sunburned man who seemed to be the one in charge. "We'd have been in real trouble if you hadn't come along. There are twenty baboons in that truck, and the lock's jammed. We'd have lost them all and the truck as well."

When he heard these words, Schmidt for the first time looked closely at his well-wishers and their vehicles; and he saw that they represented nothing less than a traveling circus—the sort of small enterprise, consisting of a few performers and fewer animals, which traveled about the Australian bush during the summer months. He recalled that a similar group had been to his town just last August. They didn't amount to much, but they were a welcome break in the lonely monotony of country living. And he had liked the animals, particularly the monkeys.

At that thought the farmer looked again toward the still smoldering truck. "I should think you'd better get those monkeys out now, lads," he said. "That smoke will do 'em no good. I've got a pair of steel shears in the cab. Let's see if they can make a dent in that padlock."

And it was no sooner said than done. The heavy metal shears easily clipped off the lock so that the heavy door to the panel truck could be opened. As it swung back, forty pairs of eyes stared out, blinking in the bright sunlight. Though grateful for a breath of fresh air, the monkeys showed little enthusiasm for setting foot outside their customary home. They huddled together just beyond the pool of sunshine.

Lindsay stuck his head in to get a better look. He'd never had much chance to see such animals up close. The baboons drew

back in panic—all but one, that is. For some unknown reason, a single small creature came slowly forward. He stood just inside the truck door looking at the surprised farmer. The monkey scratched his head; and then quite without warning walked right up to Schmidt and seized his hand in a grasp of firm friendship. The man was delighted. He had never known monkeys could be so companionable. The watching circus employees laughed heartily.

"Well, my friend, it appears you've got a buddy," said one. At that moment a thought occurred to the sheepman. "So I have, and he's a sprightly feller too," he responded, turning to the one who had spoken. "What are my chances of buying this monk? He'd make a fine pet and a good companion for a lonely man."

It was now that the gang boss took up the conversation. "Your chances of buying that beast are mighty poor, my lad, for we are going to give him to you. You saved us a truck and a bunch of animals. The least we can do is to let you have this one. Take him."

And so it was that as Lindsay Schmidt drove slowly back that afternoon along the winding, rutted road which led to his isolated farmhouse he took with him a new partner—the baboon. Johnny (for that was what Lindsay had elected to call him) sat quietly in the passenger seat gazing out across the empty lands. He had come with the farmer readily, indeed gladly; but now he seemed subdued, as though perhaps realizing for the first time that his life was changing drastically. He was leaving behind the simian companions that he knew so well, the familiar smells and sights of the circus and the strange excitement of the crowds. He did not know what lay ahead. He moved across the seat toward Lindsay and, laying his head in the farmer's lap, promptly went to sleep.

Schmidt looked down at his new charge. What had he let himself in for? After all, hadn't he come out here into the plains to get away from people? That girl back in Brisbane, whom he had loved so much, she'd left him flat. Right then he had vowed that he wouldn't get messed up with people again; getting close to them only meant getting hurt. Out here it was all so simple, just the farm and the sheep. Still, the monkey wasn't a person, even if right now he looked a lot like a baby curled up there on the seat. It was just an animal, and he knew how to handle animals. What could possibly happen that would be out of the ordinary?

Their new life together was full of surprises, not only for the baboon who had to learn to live like a human, but also for the man. Schmidt had assumed that the animal would be nothing more than a friendly and amusing pet, something to provide a little companionship and fun after the day's chores were over. Johnny proved to be a lot more than that.

In the first place, he was a big pet—a very big pet. Weighing less than ten pounds when he came to live at the farm, Johnny quickly gained weight. Within six months he was up to forty pounds, on the way to an adult weight of over eighty. Moreover, he ate just about everything his master did, being particularly fond of vegetables.

And he was fussy about where he did his eating. That first night the sheepman put his pet's bowl on the floor not far from the table and sat down to his own meal. Johnny sat for a while watching him; then he picked up his bowl and, clambering up the nearest chair, joined his master at the table. From then on they sat side by side sharing the same foods in perfect harmony.

Schmidt was rather surprised at all of this, of course. Not that he hadn't heard of the supposed intelligence of apes and baboons. He certainly knew that they were far brighter than horses and dogs; but still he hadn't really expected his companion to be sensitive as well. Clearly the simian understood not only how people ate but also that this was very different from the way in which animals were fed. The baboon wanted to be treated as an equal.

Monkey See, Monkey Do

It also soon became evident that the monkey wanted to earn his keep. He followed Schmidt around the farm watching as the man tended his garden and fed the large flock of chickens. One day when Lindsay was trying to figure out how to carry three large buckets of meal for the hens, he was startled to see his baboon grasp the odd container in both hands and wobble off toward the barn. Fascinated, the man followed him.

Johnny never hesitated in his self-appointed task. He had, after all, been seeing the job done for weeks. He went right into the chicken coop (the birds had long since gotten used to him) and quickly began to scatter the feed. Lindsay Schmidt put down the other two buckets and went off to attend to other matters. Never again would he have to feed the chickens. They were in good hands!

And as much as he liked chickens, Johnny liked sheep even more. Even when he was small, he would run about in the flock climbing atop the docile animals and even jumping from one to another when they were closely bunched together.

But the baboon quickly learned that the sheep were not pets or members of the family. He watched as they were driven to and from the fold, fed and sheared. He apparently didn't feel that any of these jobs was beyond his capacities, for he tried them all. He wasn't much good at shearing, for he couldn't get the hang of cutting with shears; but he liked to pick the burrs out of the sheeps' wool prior to shearing, and he was a whiz at that. In fact, there were few humans who could keep up with him at the task.

Johnny was also a pretty good shepherd. He was, of course, not as fast as the sheep dogs at turning a line of frightened animals, but he was a lot smarter than his canine counterparts. It was not long before Schmidt could rely on Johnny to bring in the flocks by himself. He would just take out the dogs, who treated him like another human, and direct their efforts in rounding up the animals.

By the time the monkey had been with him a year, Lindsay Schmidt was the envy of his neighborhood. Neither he nor his fellow farmers could really believe his good luck. He had brought home a pet and ended up with a hardworking and trustworthy hired man. He was indeed a happy man, but he was to have even more cause for gratitude.

One of the problems of running a large sheep spread was feeding the animals during the dry months when there was little grass on the range. At this time Lindsay had to spend long days driving from flock to flock distributing bales of hay. Since he had no hired helper, he had to both drive and throw off the feed, a slow and inefficient method.

Of course, it wasn't long before the rancher decided to see what his companion could do to help him with this task. He took the baboon out on the tractor to see how the process went.

Johnny had ridden the tractor before, and he loved it. The feeling of movement fascinated him, but even more he enjoyed watching the driver shift gears and turn the great steering wheel. And, of course, he almost immediately understood what was required concerning the bales of feed. After only half a day on the range Schmidt was able to retire to the front seat while his faithful companion cast off the mounds of baled fodder.

The work, of course, went much faster, and by late afternoon the day's task was nearly completed. The sheep rancher was delighted with his circumstances. From now on his feeding problems were solved.

Unexpectedly, though, a problem arose. Lindsay heard a noise at the rear of the tractor. When he turned, he saw the monkey struggling with a large bale whose binding had become entangled in some wiring at the back of his seat. It was a bad time for that, he thought, for they were right in the center of the largest flock, and he wanted to get all the hay out as soon as possible.

Putting the tractor into low so it was only moving about five miles per hour, the farmer stood up and turned around in order to assist his simian friend. At that moment the vehicle hit a bump. Lindsay stumbled backward, grabbed desperately for support and found none. Slowly, almost reluctantly, he toppled over the hood of the tractor and, hitting the ground, rolled down a little rise into the next gully.

Even as he fell, he was thinking of the machine and the fact that it was in gear. It would be coming right at him! He landed on his face in the dry dirt, still trying to figure out how to get out of the way. The plan, as it had formed in his mind, was to land on his feet and spring away. Unfortunately, the shock of impact was too great. Where he had thought to leap, now all he could do was crawl. And as he crawled he looked, looked far above him at the great treads and crushing weight which were coming right down on top of him. The roar of the engine was very close. There was no escape.

Just then the sound ceased. The tractor had stopped. Lindsay, there in the dust with his fingers tangled in the dry grass stems, heard the motor cut out. Someone had shut it off. Only one person (he had long since ceased to think of Johnny as an animal) could have done that. He picked himself up and walked slowly to the tractor. There in the driver's seat sat his "pet."

Johnny was sitting there very gravely, a look of concern on his intelligent face. Schmidt remembered that day long before when he had saved the baboon from the fire and how it, out of all its fellows, had known how to show its appreciation. Without hesitation, he put out his hand. His companion took it and shook it vigorously. Clearly, he too remembered.

"Well, now we are even, old fellow," said the farmer. "As far as I'm concerned you are the top man on my ranch, and I'll lick anyone who says otherwise."

Well, that really did it. Any monkey who could think like that deserved the best. Schmidt went out and got him a pair of dungarees, a couple of shirts and a straw hat just like his own.

And naturally no one had to tell the animal how to dress. He'd been watching that too for years, just waiting for a chance to put on his own clothes.

And the rancher even turned the tractor over to him. After all, as he was quite a lot smaller, Johnny couldn't really handle the bales all that well; but he could drive. Of course, at first he only went in straight lines, though he was always pretty good at dodging rocks or trees. But after a few weeks of instruction he got so he could maneuver as if he had been behind the wheel for years. He could climb on the tractor, start it up and drive off like there was nothing to it. People used to come from miles around to watch that monkey handle a tractor.

Naturally a relationship as unusual as this one couldn't help but attract attention. In fact, it got a little difficult to farm at times, what with all the outsiders running around trying to take photographs of Johnny. But there was good to come of this, too.

One day a reporter from a Sydney newspaper came by to do a story on the simian farmhand. In the course of interviewing Schmidt, he suggested, half in jest, that the rancher ought to apply for a government subsidy for his pet.

Now Lindsay knew that the Australian government gave every farmer a ninety-dollar-per-year tax deduction for every full-time employee he had. But how could that apply to a baboon? Anyway, it was worth a try; so he sent for the forms. When the farmer received these he was stunned. Nowhere on the papers was there any question that could disclose that his employee was an ape. Certainly such queries as "Age," "Name," "Time he has worked for you," presented no problem. But there was a small problem. The government required a statement from the employee. This, of course, was impossible—even for so gifted a simian as Johnny.

So Schmidt filled out the form and sent it back, along with a simple statement that since his employee was a monkey he was unable to provide a signed statement.

It was about three months later that the investigator arrived. He was the usual sort of government investigator, meaning that he snooped into everything and believed nothing. From the first it was obvious that he thought it was all a hoax. How could an ape do farm work?

Well, the rancher took him out on the land and just let him watch Johnny in action. He saw the baboon feed three hundred chickens, weed a vegetable garden, drive a tractor out on the field where he threw bales to half a hundred sheep, and finally sit down in the shade with his master to eat a lunch of sandwiches, apples and soup, washed down with a pint of beer.

The investigator didn't say much about all that. He just kept writing and shaking his head. When he went away at the end of the day, Lindsay didn't know if he would ever hear from him again, and he certainly didn't expect to get the deduction. In fact, he kind of wished the newspaperman had never suggested the whole thing.

But strange things do happen. About a month later a letter arrived from the tax department. It was short and to the point. "John Schmidt having been found qualified as a full-time employee, his employer, Lindsay Schmidt, is hereby granted the usual annual tax abatement." There was nothing at all about baboons!

The Misjudged
Mongoose

The small animal swiftly circled his much larger adversary. He was barely two feet long from the tip of his thick bushy tail to his pointed nose, and he weighed only three pounds, but he was a terrifying fighting machine. His lips curled back from rows of filelike teeth, and his thick brown hair was ruffled with rage and exertion. Mongooses hate snakes, particularly cobras; and this one was no exception.

Moreover, to the mongoose, this fight was particularly vexing, for it had been going on for weeks! Each day—in fact, several times each day—he would be dragged from the rattan box in which he was kept and goaded into attacking the great cobra. The little mammal did not understand the nature of these contests. Fighting snakes he understood very well, for almost from birth he had seen others of his kind attack and kill them for sport and food. He had, in fact, already won several such contests prior to falling into the metal trap from which he had been delivered to the hands of his present owner.

What the mongoose did not understand was why his master would not let him make an end to the fight. The cobra was large, but it was also old and fat. Its attacks were usually half-hearted (the mongoose did not know that the snake too had wearied of the game), and on numerous occasions the swift little beast had sunk his teeth into the cobra's body just behind the flat head. A swift movement and all would have been over. But, no, every time at that moment his keeper's long stick intervened, driving him from his prey. The mongoose was beginning to suspect that the man didn't really want the snake killed after all.

But the mongoose lived in hope. Perhaps this time it would be different. He sped around the snake faster and faster, wrapping the reptile in upon itself so that its darting strikes became erratic. And then, as the long body extended itself once again, the great jaws wide to kill, the mongoose leaped high into the air straight over the deadly fangs and fell upon his adversary's back. Now he would finish it. But no such luck; it happened again. The trainer's stick pressed upon him, driving him back. Pinned against a mud wall, the mongoose watched his beaten foe disappear into the conical straw basket from which it always emerged to start the engagements. No doubt it would be back. Perhaps the next time . . .

The mongoose sat back on his haunches and awaited the bit of rancid meat he had come to expect at the conclusion of each inconclusive bout. He took no notice of the ragged crowd which had gathered to watch the fight or of his keeper eagerly soliciting coins from the onlookers.

Nor, now that the spectacle was over, did the watchers pay much attention to the mongoose. There was, however, an exception. At the edge of the group stood a white man, his skin color and clothing sharply distinguishing him from his fellow spectators. He was John Connel, a merchant sailor aboard the English freighter *Athel Prince*, which lay at anchor off the coast of India. While on shore leave, Connel had chanced upon the encounter between animal and snake. He was entranced, not with the spectacle, which he found mildly disgusting, but with the grace and beauty of the mongoose. He knew something of such animals, of their great speed and agility, of their sharp teeth and unremitting hatred of snakedom; but he had never seen one in action before. It was surely the most graceful creature he had ever observed. How terrible it was to think that it would spend its life on the wretched streets of Madras fighting inconclusive battles with an overweight cobra and living on offal.

Then a thought struck the sailor. Perhaps he could buy the little animal and take it aboard ship as a pet. The small gopher-like rodents were easily tamed, and he had seen many domesticated ones in India, their native land, where they were highly regarded as watchdogs against snakes and other predators. Others aboard ship had cats, dogs or birds. Why should he not have a mongoose?

He approached the turbaned and wily-looking trainer. "Man, I am interested in buying that wretched animal," he said, gesturing toward the mongoose, who at the sound of his voice raised his head and looked curiously at the speaker.

A sly look came into the Indian's eyes. "Oh, master, this is a very rare animal and hard to train. Without it I could not do my act. It would be very expensive."

The Englishman smiled. He knew something of Indian merchants as well as mongooses. "These beasts are as common in your country as rats are in mine," he responded. "Nor do they need to be trained to fight snakes. They are born to it. You could get a dozen as good as this one tomorrow if you wished to. I will give you a pound for it."

If the keeper was taken aback by all this, he gave no sign of it. He simply continued to extol the virtues of this particular mongoose. Shrewdly guessing that the sailor planned to keep him as a pet, something often done in India, for the animals are great ratters, he switched tactics. "He is very tame and will love you, master; all are not so gentle. I will need at least three pounds for him," he concluded.

The sailor reached into his pocket and extracted two pounds. "Here you are, fellow. We will split the difference, and the animal goes with me today."

The trainer took the money and tucked it into his robes. The mongoose watched as the two men, so different in appearance, approached. He could sense that his life was about to change.

And, of course, it was true that things were very different on the ship, for both the mongoose and John Connel. The animal liked his new existence. The food was much better, and he had a whole cabin to himself. The sailor, on the other hand, found that his fellow crewmen were not pleased with his acquisition. They had heard exaggerated stories about the mongoose and had confused the beast's prowess as a snake and rat killer with a general animus against all living things. Such was not the case, of course, for the little creatures will dwell peacefully with other pets. The sailors, however, were willing to take no chances; and they made it clear that there would be war if the new arrival decided to snack on their pets. John could not even take his friend for a stroll on the upper deck without getting dirty looks from angry bird and cat owners. Even those with small dogs were concerned!

It became evident that Connel was going to have to keep his animal in the cabin at all times. Even though the mongoose had harmed no one, the old prejudices were just too strong. And living full time with a mongoose had its problems. Though the little beast was rapidly becoming domesticated and was clearly fond of his new master, he was still a wild animal and a mischief maker. His sharp teeth could cut easily through leather or cloth; and when bored, as it often was alone in the cabin, the mongoose didn't hesistate to tear up anything within reach. Connel became accustomed to living in a shambles.

In the meantime, the freighter had made the long voyage across the Pacific and, after passing through the Panama Canal, had started north again along the Atlantic coast of North America. By this time the sailor had decided to rid himself of his pet.

But how, that was the problem. Not surprisingly, no one on the ship wanted it, and the few seamen from other vessels whom he approached were equally uninterested. Monkeys and parrots were one thing, but a killer mongoose, never!

Fortunately, when the ship docked at Duluth, Minnesota, after a voyage through the St. Lawrence Seaway, an opportunity presented itself. Now Duluth is a long way from India, and perhaps the prejudicial tales of mongoose behavior hadn't traveled this far. Also, the city had a zoo, and that zoo didn't have a mongoose. What Connel didn't know, however, was that no American zoo had a mongoose and for a very good reason. It was against the law to import or own them in this country!

However, neither the seaman nor, as it turned out, the zoo administrators were aware of this legal technicality; and when Connel and his pet arrived at the Duluth Zoo the director was delighted to see them. The mongoose also seemed delighted to see the director. He climbed out of the cramped box in which he had traveled and sat demurely on a table looking about him. He liked the smells and the hint of open spaces beyond the walls. It could be much nicer than that tiny cabin on the ship. He rubbed his head against the director's arm. That did it. Of course the zoo would be glad to accept the donation!

Connel practically ran back to the ship. He was glad that it was sailing tomorrow; hopefully before the mongoose started tearing things up or (and he shuddered at the thought) eating things up. In the meantime, though, there was little time to think of such things, for he was basking in the glory of his deed. Men who hadn't spoken to him in six months came up to shake his hand and offer to buy him a drink. Everyone was pleased that the mongoose was gone. They felt as if a curse had been lifted.

And, though they didn't know it, the curse had come to light on the officials of the Duluth Zoo. At first, however, it seemed as though they had been blessed. The mongoose was adorable and adjusted rapidly to his new life. They built a special little area for him and proudly announced in all the local newspapers that they had a rare Herpestes specimen. In response to the notices, hundreds of people flocked to the zoo to see the friendly little mammal. Children particularly were fond of him and his playful antics, and soon whole classes of schoolchildren were coming to admire the new arrival. Attendance boomed, and the zoo looked forward to new grants and more publicity. What the administration got instead was trouble, big trouble.

It seems that customs officials also read newspapers, and when the customs collector for the port of Duluth read about the mongoose he decided to take a look at what the law books said about him. He found just what he expected to find. Federal law absolutely forbade the importation or harboring of such animals. Well, it wasn't long before the collector appeared at the zoo office, statute book in hand. He probably figured that the director would just hand over the animal and that would be the end of it.

But, of course, things are hardly ever that easy. The mongoose was the biggest attraction the zoo had ever had, and the administrators weren't about to give it up so easily. Of course, a quick check with the city attorney confirmed that the collector was right in his interpretation of the law, but the zoo had other weapons.

A few calls to local and regional newspapers produced a flock of reporters all smelling a highly salable humanitarian story with a helpless and appealing victim and a suitable villain, the U.S. government. The next morning when the collector, still awaiting the arrival of the doomed animal (he had given the zoo forty-eight hours to hand it over), opened the paper he found himself featured as a heartless beast bent on destroying an innocent creature through blind adherence to an ancient and outmoded law. There were even pictures of school kids crying outside the mongoose's cage! The collector's wife stopped speaking to him. He began to get obscene phone calls.

But two can play those games. The customs bureau counterattacked. The department called in a biologist (not a Duluth resident, of course) who pointed out that the law had a purpose. Mongooses breed like rabbits, have no natural enemies other than men and domestic dogs. Moreover, where they had been introduced into countries to which they were not native, such as the islands of Trinidad and Jamaica, they had soon become nuisances. It was one thing for the little predators to eat up the rats for whose extinction they had been employed. It was quite another when they ran out of rats. The biologist raised the specter of a million raging mongooses sweeping across Minnesota devouring rabbits, squirrels, songbirds and even pet cats!

The argument was pretty appealing to some (especially the hunters who wanted to kill the rabbits and squirrels themselves), and a lot of wind went out of the zoo's sails. Of course, the director did point out that what they had was not a million mongooses but just one, an immature male who was not likely to have much chance to reproduce.

By now the deadline to surrender the fearsome beast had passed, so the collector brought in the U.S. Fish and Wildlife Service, since its agents had the police authority to physically seize the mongoose. But when the federal officers entered the zoo, they were confronted by city policemen. Both sides were now in too deep to back off, and a real federal-state conflict was brewing, all over a three-pound carnivore.

At this point the whole story broke in the national press. It was 1962, and the '60s concern with human rights was readily transferred to animal rights. Nearly all the articles which appeared were pro-mongoose, anti-customs. Seizing on this national attention, the zoo's supporters next initiated a petition drive, and within days the streets of Duluth were filled with hundreds of schoolchildren bearing petitions urging that authorities spare the animal.

Typical of these kids was Johnny Andrews. Johnny was ten and the proud owner of two cats and a beagle dog, but he loved the mongoose too. He'd been among the first to visit it at the zoo and had become hopelessly enamored of the brown squirrel-like creature. He couldn't understand why those government people wanted to kill "his mongoose," but he knew one thing. He wasn't going to let them get away with it.

That was why he carried petitions, posted handwritten notices on bulletin boards and even tried to get his parents to join him in picketing the local federal office building. But the best thing he did was to organize that "cry in." The press had really loved that—twenty kids, all howling and hanging on to the bars of the mongoose's cage. Of course, Johnny didn't really cry. He was too big for that; but he had an eye for publicity, and he figured that no one would really notice how he was faking it. He was right. His whole gang was down at the zoo, and they all had a grand time wailing and carrying on. It may not have been as effective in the long run as contacting senators and getting names on petitions, but it was sure a lot more fun.

Coinciding with the petition drive was a letter-writing campaign directed at federal officials who had the power to intervene. Thousands of letters poured in to the offices of bureau chiefs and cabinet officers, even the President of the United States. And, where possible, these officials were contacted directly. The mayor of Duluth spoke to his old friend Hubert Humphrey, then senior U.S. senator from Minnesota; and he, in turn, contacted Stewart Udall, the Secretary of the Interior. Udall unquestionably had the power to prevent seizure of the animal; whether he would exert his authority or not remained to be seen.

Superficially the politicians' choice seemed foreordained. On one side were arrayed tens of thousands of their own constituents, young and old, all clamoring for them to spare the life of a tiny creature which only under the most unlikely circumstances could ever pose a threat to anyone or anything. On the other side was a faceless bureaucracy which in its inept handling of the situation had aroused that ire against authority which lurks in the heart of every citizen. A vote for the mongoose would mean approval from those whose vote ultimately counts. A vote against would never be forgiven.

Yet, the Secretary of the Interior wavered, and with some reason. He was under great pressure not only from high officials in the affected departments, but also from others throughout the system. They perceived the whole thing as an attack on the system, their system, and on authority, their authority. If things were to get done, they had to be done in an orderly manner and through following the rules. If the citizens of Duluth could get an exemption from federal law for their mongoose, why couldn't other such exemptions be claimed for other causes by other groups? Where would it all stop?

And, of course there was the undeniable fact that large groups of mongooses could, under certain circumstances, be harmful to the environment. But, as the animal's supporters were quick to point out, so could elephants, large snakes and hundreds of other exotic creatures. That didn't prevent their being safely housed in properly safeguarded zoos. The bureaucrats didn't have much response to that one.

For months the verbal and tactical battle raged, and fortunes, like those of war, ebbed and flowed. At one point an order of seizure was issued and federal agents headed for the zoo. They were forestalled by a hastily obtained court order. At another juncture it appeared as though Secretary Udall had verbally committed himself to survival; then nothing further happened.

But the citizen groups never gave up. They continued the campaign. If enthusiasm waned, there were always more children to be photographed weeping before the mongoose's cage. They wouldn't go away.

And, in a very real way, the mongoose taught, or perhaps retaught, us a lesson in basic democracy—not to give up. The citizens really do have the power to decide. According to the Constitution it rests in them, and they can exercise it; but it is more convenient for the politicians and the bureaucrats if they do not exercise it. If, however, the people make it clear that they will not be denied, their elected and appointed officials eventually have nothing to say. They must yield. And that is just what happened at long last in Duluth.

There came a day when the men in the big offices decided that there was nothing to be gained by fighting or stalling. The cost in time, money and public good will far outweighed the questionable and seemingly unobtainable benefit of teaching "those troublemakers" a lesson. Prudence dictated a retreat before more harm was done. The word was passed. Within hours Secretary Udall announced quietly (it wasn't, after all, a major policy decision) that an exemption to the law might be made for good cause as shown in the case of the Duluth mongoose. The law was, of course, wise and proper and to be obeyed; but as the animal in question was to spend its natural life in an escape-proof cage, any great potential harm that it might do was not likely to result. Accordingly, he might live.

It was no coincidence that among the great crowd who celebrated the victory in the Duluth Zoo there were many who carried flags and banners including those which bore the well-known slogan "Don't Tread on Me!" The mongoose had taken his place alongside Paul Revere, Nathan Hale and those other great patriots who stood up to despots!

A Fish with a Mind
of His Own

The first thing that the salmon saw were the shark's jaws. The monster was hurtling through the school of smaller fish like a runaway express train, his huge mouth open wide to inhale a meal. Though he had never seen a white shark before, the salmon intuitively knew that it spelled danger. He crash-dived, plunging straight down into the green depths of the northern Pacific. It was a close call. The white came so near that his churning tail actually brushed the salmon's side, knocking him end over end.

But now the great shark was gone as suddenly as he had come, and the school of salmon reassembled, its ranks once more diminished by a natural calamity. His own momentary fright passed; the young salmon did not brood long on what had happened. Something which would seem to us to be a terrible experience was to him a part of the daily routine. He swam, he slept, he pursued the smaller fish which were his prey, and he was in turn pursued. It was a way of life, and he knew no other.

In fact, the fish lived almost entirely in the present. True, he had learned some things—vital things: which creatures to eat, which to avoid, how to seek the proper temperature level, when to leave the surface if a storm threatened. But these things were matters almost of instinct. Of his own history, his lifetime of nearly two years' duration, he remembered almost nothing.

It was an interesting life, though not unlike that experienced by many of his fellows. He was a silver salmon, one of the larger anadromous fish native to the West Coast of North America. Like all salmon, he had been born in fresh water, yet it was his destiny to live most of his life in the sea, returning to fresh water only to spawn.

Now, salmon are highly thought of, both in Europe and the United States, for their eating and sporting qualities. So between commercial and sport fishermen, their numbers have been greatly reduced over the years. As a result, fish hatcheries have been established where young salmon can be raised for release in the Pacific and Atlantic oceans. Our salmon was born in one of these, the Prairie Creek Hatchery near Eureka in northern California. He was hatched from a fertilized egg in a spawning tub and when about an inch long was transferred to a larger tank where he was fed on chopped liver and allowed to grow until he was about a half foot long.

Though he didn't know it, of course, the salmon was now ready to begin his travels. On a spring day in 1962 he was suddenly lifted from the water in a dip net and grasped in a rubber-clad hand. A hatchery attendant turned him on his back and with a deft movement clipped a bit of flesh from one of his fins. He was now marked and could thus be recognized if and when he returned from his migration, for scientists have studied the habits of the silver salmon and have learned that when released in western coastal streams, they will travel out into the northern Pacific, feeding and growing as they journey along the southern coast of Alaska and as far west as Siberia. This trip takes several years and covers thousands of miles; and at its end the salmon, now fully mature, return to the very streams in which they were stocked. There they spawn and create a new generation. But the perils, disease, storms and natural predators

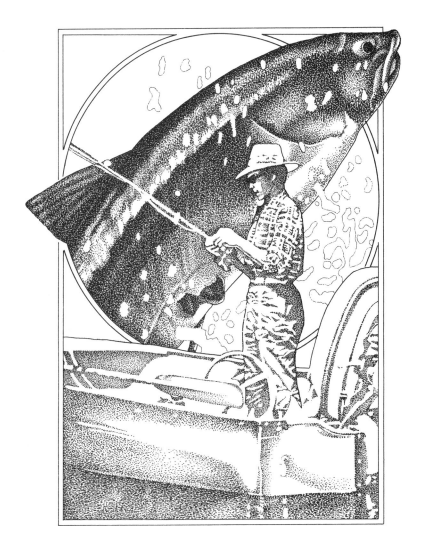

which they face along the way are many; and research has shown that no more than three of any ten tagged or marked salmon survive to complete this amazing journey.

Would this salmon be one of the fortunate ones? Only time would tell. Certainly his eventual destiny was of little concern to him on that day when he was, along with hundreds of his fellows, poured from a milk can into a coastal river not far from Eureka. His only thought at that moment was to find a rock to hide under!

But the small fish soon lost his fear of the new surroundings and began to feed. He also began to move gradually downstream. As he approached the ocean, he sensed for the first time the odor and taste of salt water. A strange, ancient desire stirred in him. The group of swimming salmon drew together, for all felt the same commitment to the unknown; and as a group they moved out into the Pacific. Instinctively they traveled north and west, against the prevailing currents. They had no specific destination that they knew of, yet they were drawn irresistibly onward.

Day by day, week by week, month by month, the fish swam, feeding and being fed upon. The thousands dwindled to hundreds, but the remaining ones grew larger, stronger and wiser in the ways of the deep. They encountered sharks and, in the cold seas north of Japan, nets. The young silver saw the net first—a huge gray curtain moving swiftly through the water, its edges slowly curving in upon themselves. The school recognized its peril and bore for the bottom. But this trick which had often succeeded with larger fish failed with the new adversary. The salmon's descent was blocked by the net's great cuplike bottom. The trap was closing inexorably. Up again, through the chill green waters, they raced until they flashed free of the water in a shower of silver. Then, skipping across the surface, they sought for a low point in the encircling net. Everywhere it seemed closed and held high by buoys. Was there no escape? The fishermen saw their efforts and smiled in satisfaction. This would be a good catch indeed. But it was not to be so. On the far side of the trap a buoy dragged in the strong current and broke loose. The net sagged a few inches below the surface. The school of salmon found the gap. In a body they sped to it and streamed through, running like silver coins through the hands of their would-be captors.

On they went. Nearly two years had now passed since he entered the ocean, and the young salmon was over a foot long. His body was maturing; and the age-old desire to spawn—to mate and to reproduce his kind—began to kindle in him. A similar need was felt by the other members of the school, and almost as one they turned east once more. Drawn by instinct, by smell or perhaps a combination of both, they headed unerringly for the little river in which they had been stocked. As the months passed, they grew larger but gradually came to eat less as their whole beings became directed toward a single goal—to spawn.

The fish were within a few miles of the California coast when yet another danger presented itself. A veritable fleet of small boats, each containing several sports fishermen, blocked the way to the river. They too understood the salmon's need, and they waited at the river's mouth. The fishing boats moved slowly back and forth across the estuary trolling long lines to which were attached baits and lures of various kinds—whatever experience had shown would interest or enrage a spawning salmon.

As the school felt the first hint of fresh water mingling with the salt, they also encountered the first lures. Many fish passed them by, but not all. Something silvery flashed across the young salmon's field of vision. It fluttered in the water, rising and falling almost like an injured minnow. Breaking away from the group, he followed it. Something warned him that all was not right. The movement was strange, unlike that of any fish he had ever seen. Yet it was enticing and annoying. It made him furious to see this bold little thing flipping and flopping across his path. He would teach it a lesson. Swiftly he pursued the intruder, and with a powerful flip of his tail he fell upon it. His strong jaws closed, but on what? This was no fish or other living thing. It was hard and cold; and, worse yet, he could not seem to let go of it. When he opened his mouth to spit out the strange object, it clung to his jaw. It was, in fact, hooked to him.

Just then the fish felt a new and terrifying sensation. The tiny creature, far stronger than he could have imagined, was now pulling at him, trying to draw him upward through the water. The salmon turned his broad side to the surface and headed for the depths.

Above, in a circling motorboat, a young boy turned to his father. "I've got one, Dad. I can feel him," he cried.

"Good going, but take your time," his father replied. "He's down deep, and he'll tear loose if you reel too fast. From the way your rod's bent, he isn't going to be very big, so you shouldn't have too much trouble with him."

Down below, the tiring salmon was having lots of trouble. His strength and weight, barely two pounds, were no match for the strong line and heavy rod. He dove this way and that, but nothing availed. Slowly but surely he felt himself drawn toward the boat. But suddenly he saw another way. If he couldn't go down, he would go up. Summoning all his strength, he headed for the water's surface like a bullet shot from a gun. In the boat the boy suddenly felt his line go slack.

"He's gone, Dad," he said, and he let the rod hang loose in his hand. But his father was wiser in the ways of fish.

"No, he's not. He's going to jump," he cried. "Reel like the devil or he'll get too much slack." But the warning came too late. Up and out came the salmon. Within a scant ten yards of the boat he arched from the water shaking his head savagely. The hated metal lure snapped in his jaw and tore loose sailing across the surface. The exhausted fish fell back. He was free.

The salmon was hurt and terrified and alone, for all of his kin who had escaped the fishermen had now entered the home river. His instinct was to follow them, yet pain and fright prevented him. He could not bring himself to enter the stream, for that would require passing once more through the barrier of fishing boats.

Scientists do not know what it is that brings the salmon back to their natal waters. Some feel that it is a highly developed sense of smell, others that it is caused by a form of sensory imprint, a "road map," as it were, in the fish's head. Whatever the cause, the pull is strong but not incontrovertible; and in this case, as in others, events altered the instinctual mechanism.

Denied access to his home river, the salmon sought another, for his need to spawn remained undiminished. He moved slowly down the coast, and a few miles farther on found a larger stream. It was broad and flat and warm, quite unsuitable for salmon who require clear, cold waters. Yet the fish felt himself strongly drawn to it and not by the spawning need alone. Somehow in these waters he felt closer to "home" than he had even at the mouth of the river where he had been released two years before.

He entered, crossed a sandbar and swam upstream. The unusual warmth of the water bothered him. He grew sluggish and traveled more slowly. His respiration was slowing down, and though he did not know it he was close to death. A few degrees higher and he would not be able to breathe. He would die in that muddy stream.

Then suddenly a hint of cooler, fresher water reached him; and, more than refreshment, the current carried a message intended for him alone. The salmon turned aside. On the north side of the river a small creek entered. Cold and clear, it tumbled down a narrow gorge into the larger stream. The salmon swam without hesitation straight to the creek mouth. The water felt wonderful, and the scent that drew him was stronger. On he went.

The little stream wound its way through high bushes and past open fields. Here were deep pools where the fish rested; there, shallows filled with gravel across which he practically crawled with his upper body half out of the water. Once a great highway crossed the stream, and the fish entered a dark culvert which carried the stream beneath the road. Dozens of cars and trucks passed above, but none of their occupants saw the slim silver form which slipped quietly past below them.

The water sheltered only a few other creatures—frogs, tiny minnows and a few water spiders—but these did not concern him. Nothing in the stream could challenge him. What he feared lay without. Used to seeking safety in the depths, he wisely feared the shallows. And well he might, for danger there was. As he crossed a wide sandy flat, a shadow fell upon him. A great hawk swooped low, its talons reaching for his head. Using his tail like a paddle, the salmon flipped himself end over end into deeper water, soaking his startled adversary and gaining his freedom. After that he did not linger in the shallows.

Several miles above the river a ditch which drained farmland entered the creek. Though cool, its waters were thick with sediment. Still, it bore the scent. Without hesitation, the fish left his creek for its dubious comfort. The drainage canal was flat and shallow and afforded little protection. He would be prey to every bird and animal that sought fish flesh. The salmon sensed that this was no place to tarry. Faster he swam. The drainage ditch was joined by another. His instinct told him to go that way. The second ditch was, if anything, even shallower than the first. The sun beat down on the warm water. A mud bar blocked his way. Gathering himself together like a snake, he churned across it into the deeper water beyond.

A wandering fox came upon the odd track in the mud. He could make nothing of it, but it interested him. He started trotting slowly upstream following the salmon's path.

Not knowing he was pursued, the fish still hurried on. Suddenly the ditch ended in a deep round pool. Above it loomed four identical black pipes, and from each gushed a stream of cold water. The salmon showed no hesitation. Somehow he knew that the pipe on the far right was the correct one. He swam to it and leaped three feet through the air into its mouth. The flow of water knocked him back. He finned slowly about the pool preparing for a second attempt.

A few feet away the bushes parted at the water's edge. The fox appeared. He had never seen a salmon before, but it looked like it could be eaten. He headed for the pool. Just then the fish leaped again, and this time his powerful tail caught the lip of the pipe and drove him into it. Swimming almost vertically, the silver thrashed up the four-inch-wide cylinder. Three feet up, there was a right-angle turn. Rolling on his side and bending almost double, he navigated it.

Now swimming horizontally again, the salmon came to the end of the pipe. His way was barred by a wire grill. He backed off and hurled himself at it. It did not move. Again and again the fish butted the grill. His head grew raw from the impact. Then unexpectedly the screening gave way, and, propelled by his own efforts, the fish hurtled out of the pipe and down into a flat pool. For a few minutes he paddled slowly around getting his bearings; then, with a feeling of absolute certainty, he made his final move. Arching out of the water, he cleared a wire mesh net and dropped into the adjoining pool. It was a breeding tank—the very one in which he had been born. The silver salmon had come home at last to the Prairie Creek Hatchery!

Namu—Killer Whale

George Henderson was angry, very angry. That net was stuck on the bottom again! Henderson was a commercial fisherman, the captain of a large coastal fishing boat based at Namu in British Columbia. He and his crew continually braved the cold rough waters of the northern Pacific in search of mackerel, hake and similar fish. Generally they did well, but twice this week their great drag net had become entangled in debris on the ocean floor, resulting in hours of wasted time and, in one case, extensive damage to the equipment. Now it had happened again.

Henderson swung the boat around to take strain off the tackle. They would have to raise as much of the net as possible before they began to free it. "John," he called to his winch man, "start bringing her up."

"Aye," John Robertson replied as he started the machinery which would pull the heavy net off the bottom.

For a few moments nothing was heard but the whirr of the motor and the creak of winches, then Robertson spoke again. "Captain, the net is moving about. It is rising faster than we are reeling. I think there is something in it, something big." There was now a note of alarm in the seaman's voice.

Nor did the captain have long to dwell on this new develop-
ment, for almost at once a thrashing form broke the surface and
vaulted six feet into the air in an effort to free itself from the
thousands of pounds of line which clung to it. As the creature
hung momentarily against the sky, Henderson glimpsed a great
pectoral fin and the stark black-on-white color scheme which
belongs to only one being on God's earth—the killer whale!
They had caught the last thing they could possibly have wanted.

The crew peered over the side at the beast which, now
strangely quiet, lay alongside their boat. At twelve feet in length,
he was nearly half the size the boat was; yet he was not yet full
grown. He was, however, quite large enough for them.

Everyone aboard knew well the tales of the killer whale's
cruel and terrible appetite: how it would throw young sea lions
into the air like rubber balls before eating them, how it could
engulf a whole school of fish in its enormous maw. This was not
the sort of catch they had hoped for, and they would gladly
have released it. Unfortunately, they could not.

The whale was hopelessly enveloped in the heavy mesh of the
fishing net. He could not escape, nor could his captors free it on
the open sea. Fate had bound them together.

George Henderson reluctantly abandoned the day's fishing.
He would have to settle for this unexpected and fearsome catch.
The boat swung about and headed back to port. The whale,
who somehow seemed almost to understand the situation, swam
easily alongside.

The vessel moored just off Namu, and it was soon surrounded by boats filled with scores of curious onlookers, all
come to see the great killer. Henderson became nervous. What
if the creature became upset and started to thrash around? People might be hurt or even killed. He had thought to release the
catch alive, but now it looked safer to kill him. He went below
for a rifle.

Upon returning to the deck, the captain learned that he had
received a radio message. Somehow, American scientists had

already learned of the captive and wanted him—alive. They were prepared to pay a goodly sum and to send a special vessel for him. Suddenly everything had changed. The crew was jubilant. There was going to be some profit in this venture after all. They quickly set about posting a watch to keep spectators at a safe distance. The monster had become an asset.

When the people from the United States arrived, they were delighted with the killer whale. He was exactly what they wanted, not too large but mature enough to survive on his own. The only question remaining was how to get the giant mammal back home. And they also had an idea about that. The scientists arranged for the making of a giant structural steel cage which could be towed behind a fishing boat.

After some maneuvering the trapped whale was removed from the fishing net and transferred to the traveling cage. All during this operation the creature remained surprisingly docile. He had, in fact, already shown considerable interest in and affection for his human captors, particularly since they had begun to feed him.

Accordingly, the scientists, who had decided to take the mammal to Seattle, Washington, anticipated little problem in the transfer. And indeed things at first went quite smoothly. The specially designed trawler moved swiftly south, and the captive (now named Namu) followed obediently behind in his submerged cage.

But on the second morning out an unexpected problem arose. About ten o'clock the engineer reported that something had struck the hull of the boat. Soon other and similar blows could be felt, and within moments the attackers could be seen. A school of several killer whales were circling the vessel and butting it from all sides. Simultaneously, a jerking on the lines leading to the cage made it clear that it too was under assault. The intention of the dolphins seemed clear. They wanted to sink the trawler and destroy the cage in which Namu was imprisoned!

The crew of the fishing vessel was more than a little concerned. Though it seemed unlikely that the creatures could make the kind of concerted assault that could capsize the boat, it was possible that their constant battering might spring a plate or two; and the consequences of that could be disastrous. Moreover, if the cage came loose, its living cargo would sink without hope.

The situation was, to say the least, an uncomfortable one. Some of the crew were for trying to shoot the attackers—until wiser heads reminded them that a wounded killer whale is one of the most dangerous creatures on earth. Another group proposed to cast off the cage, for there was little doubt that it was what the enemy sought. The scientists, naturally, would not hear of this; but they, on the other hand, were singularly lacking in practical solutions to what was becoming a major problem.

Fortunately, however, Namu took things into his own hands, or rather fins. Electronic receivers aboard the trawler suddenly began to pick up a series of high-pitched whistles emanating from the iron cage. Namu was talking! Almost immediately the school of killer whales gave up their attack on the vessel and, gathering around the imprisoned creature, began to respond in a like manner. For a few minutes the boat's communications system was overwhelmed by a veritable avalanche of sound. Then, as suddenly as it had begun, the conversation ended. And with its ending came the departure of the killer whales. They slid silently out of sight, leaving the vessel to proceed without hindrance. There was not a man aboard who doubted that they owed their deliverance to Namu.

And, of course, to the remarkable social behavior of dolphins. For many years sailors and fishermen have been aware that these mammals not only travel in groups with clearly defined social relationships and leadership roles, but that they will also, where possible, take action to assist others of their kind who are in difficulty. This, naturally, was what had led them to attack the trawler.

On the other hand, scientists now also know that dolphins

have some ability to communicate among themselves. This was quite evident in the present incident. Namu, for whatever reason, had simply told the other whales that he did not need help and that they should leave the trawler alone. Perhaps he understood that the attackers could not really help him. Perhaps he just wanted to see where his human captors were taking him. In any case, no more killer whales hindered the boat's southward passage.

It was midsummer 1965 when the killer whale reached Seattle. Long before his arrival, it had been decided that Namu would be housed in an inlet of the great bay which adjoined the city. In preparation for this an iron mesh net had been strung across the mouth of the inlet, effectively preventing escape.

Namu always seemed quite content with this arrangement. Upon being released from the cage, he had swum swiftly about the inlet, examining it thoroughly. This done, the huge creature slid leisurely up to the nearest dock and, sticking his head above water, he began to whistle. It didn't take anyone very long to figure out what Namu wanted. He was hungry! A few fresh salmon were quickly procured, and the new arrival gobbled them down with evident gusto.

The incident with the fish gave the scientists an idea. If Namu would "sing for his supper," so to speak, was it possible that he would also talk to them as he had to the other killer whales? Recording equipment was procured, and for several weeks every sound that Namu made was carefully preserved. Then, after playing the material back several times, it was possible for a technician to mimic the noises. The end result was certainly some of the strangest communications ever made. The scientists would send whole strings of bleeps and whistles out to Namu; he, with evident enthusiasm, would respond in even more complex patterns. It was the first real communication between man and beast. There was just one problem. To this day, only one party, the whale, knows what was being said!

And perhaps it was all just a game to Namu; for early in his captivity he showed that he loved to play. Contrary to the behavior of his kind in the wild, he proved a docile, if high spirited, pet. He enjoyed the usual seal games—catching and throwing a ball, swimming and diving—but he seemed to prefer more complex activities. It soon became evident that while eating, for example, was pleasurable, it was more fun if it involved sport. Thus, if his raw fish were hidden or placed in a difficult spot, he would delight in retrieving them. The great mammal also loved to have his stomach scratched and would gladly turn on his back to allow this at every opportunity.

After a few months of this, one of the younger and more daring scientists began to wonder just how fond Namu was of men, how far would he let them go before the great jaws closed. It was a dangerous game, but he decided to risk it. So early one morning the young man, whose name was Todd Anderson, slid quietly into the bay right next to the dock where Namu was having breakfast.

At first the great beast showed little interest in the tiny human so boldly swimming about him; then, when he had finished eating, Namu turned swiftly and reared above the startled man. Those watching from the dock gasped in horror. They sensed impending tragedy. Instead, they got comedy. Coming down abruptly just a few feet away, the whale showered his prey with water! This was just the first of a whole bag of tricks.

It turned out that Namu was absolutely delighted to have a companion; and though he seemed at times disappointed by his playmate's limited ability to swim and dive, he was always ready to race or play water tag. And he seemed to have absolutely no fear of human contact. Not only did he like being scratched, but he was even willing to serve as a form of aquatic horse. Anderson discovered this one day when he decided to see if he could climb aboard Namu while the whale was taking a little nap. Whether or not Namu was really asleep no one will ever know, but one thing is clear: as soon as the man had climbed up on his back and grasped his great pectoral fin the whale took off. Round and round the bay he raced, reaching speeds of thirty miles per hour, while his desperate cargo clung helplessly to an uncertain perch. But all ended well with the giant eventually coming to a stop right against the dock and waiting patiently while his passenger disembarked. And this was just the beginning. From then on Namu delighted in taking anyone who was willing to go for breathtaking rides around the bay.

It was evident, though, that Todd Anderson was the whale's real favorite. Others were mostly ignored or their offerings of food and frolic politely accepted, but the sight of Anderson on the dock sent the whale into paroxysms of delight. He would roll on his back, leap out of the water or go through a whole battery of other tricks to display his enthusiasm and to induce his friend to climb aboard for a ride or, at least, to pat his half-submerged head. There was no doubt that the killer whale could distinguish among his keepers and that from among them he had selected one upon whom to lavish his affections.

Moreover, almost from the first, it had been evident that the whale was very intelligent. Not only could he learn to take directions, but, more important, he could reason on his own. There was, for example, the incident with the motorboat. A group of visitors out for a ride in the bay stopped to scratch Namu's belly. Rolling on his back, he gradually worked his way deeper in the water until he was below the small boat. Then, quite without warning, he rose to the surface again, this time with the boat on his stomach. The passengers grabbed for everything in sight, but it really wasn't necessary. Namu, apparently anticipating that the small vessel would slide off his stomach, had raised a fin on each side, effectively protecting it. This done, he proceeded to swim sedately about the bay, looking something like a small sidewheel steamer.

Nor did the killer whale content himself with human companionship. One morning attendants arriving to feed him could find no evidence of his presence in his usual haunts. However, their transmitters were alive with squeaks and whistles. Namu was at the edge of the great iron net. On the other side were two of his kin. They were carrying on an animated conversation. Thereafter, it was not unusual for one or more of the creatures to visit the inlet each day. Having once discovered Namu, they seemed to make his home a regular stopping place on their travels up and down the Pacific coast.

Namu, meanwhile, grew and prospered. He soon reached a weight of over six tons, and his strength was absolutely amazing. He could leap ten to twelve feet straight up out of the water and, as previously mentioned, easily bear a sixteen-foot motorboat and three passengers on his stomach. His eyesight was remarkable, and he possessed the same sonar ability common in the smaller members of the dolphin family. He was, in short, a most unusual creature.

But, of course, like all of us, the giant mammal had faults and weaknesses. He was never mean or violent, though; if teased, he would grumble with annoyance and take refuge in deeper water. But he was a glutton, and worse yet, he was incurably nosy. It was, in fact, his curiosity that eventually proved his undoing.

Namu had always been curious about the net which blocked his way to the open ocean. Perhaps it was a desire to return to the wild, perhaps only the attentiveness he showed toward everything about him. Whatever the case, the great creature was often found hovering near the steel barrier. This was particularly true just after a visit from his wild kin.

It was, in fact, after just such a visit that Namu tried the net for the last time. He had long been frustrated by the strange steel barrier that denied him access to his kin and the deep water in which they swam so freely. Now once again memory of the open sea stirred in the leviathan, and he swam slowly to the wall. As always, it resisted his efforts. It could not be broken through or pushed aside.

The killer whale sank slowly to the bottom of the bay, nosing carefully along the lower edge of the metal grid. Instinctively he knew that it must have a weak spot. And he found it. Close to the outer edge of the great arc there was an upward bulge in the wall where it rose over a small mound on the sea bed. At that point there was a gap, just a few feet, between the bottom and the metal.

Without hesitation the whale drove himself into the opening, his great fins churning the sea bottom to a thick brown mush. In and under he went—five, then ten feet—almost halfway. Then he stuck. The iron closed fast against his straining back. He could move neither forward nor backward.

Namu reared in fear against the great weight that was pressing down upon him. He was a mammal and would soon need to replenish his air supply. He sensed that there was little time left. He was right.

The attendants found their charge the next morning forty feet down in the clear water, still wedged hopelessly beneath the steel barrier. He had lived with men, learned from them and taught them; but in the end his need to be with his own kind had proven too strong. It had led him to his death.

Steeplechase

Moifaa half turned in his narrow stall, trying instinctively to face the winds raging about him. He was a big rawboned horse, standing nearly six feet at the shoulders, and he was cramped in his boxlike quarters. He was also terrified. Not only was he in a place totally strange to him—the deck of a ship—but now something worse was happening. The gentle roll of the deck to which he had gradually become accustomed (unnatural though it was to one whose life had been spent on solid ground) had been replaced by a violent heaving and swaying. The sky had grown black, and great waves surged across the deck, drenching the horse. He was cold and wet and very hungry, for the storm was so violent that no man dared to bring him food across the waste of water which separated the ship's cabin and the makeshift stable.

But, bad as things might have seemed to Moifaa, they were actually far worse. The ship was beginning to sink! Two days before, as it rounded the Cape of Good Hope, off southern Africa, the steamer had run into a raging storm. The captain tried to reach the nearest port, but early on the second day a massive wave brought down the smokestack, putting out the ship's fires and leaving it at the mercy of the sea. The heavy stack lay like a millstone across the port side of the stricken vessel forcing that area down into the water. All day the crew labored to cut away the smokestack; and at dusk they finally succeeded, but at a terrible cost. For as the massive chimney slid into the deep, it bore with it the ship's carpenter and two seamen. Their companions watched helplessly as the doomed men disappeared into the storm clinging to the foundering wreckage. In a way, perhaps, these men were fortunate. They at least died without learning that their labors were in vain.

And vain they were, for the danger which they had fought to avert had already come to pass. While the ship had been listing under the weight of the battered stack, its cargo had begun to shift. First a trunk, then a box, then a drum of oil broke loose and began to slide about deep in the hold. Each time the ship rolled, these objects hurtled across the cargo spaces like cannonballs, crashing into other objects and breaking them loose. Seamen who went below to try to bind down the cargo were crushed beneath it like flies, and eventually the lower decks of the steamer resembled a great bowling alley with thousands of tons of merchandise crashing against the steel sides of the stricken ship.

As the steamer wallowed in the mountain-high waves, the loose cargo pounded its sides without letup. The result was inevitable. Under the constant battering, the steel plates began to give way. Here and there a bolt popped loose, and a crack appeared. A trickle of water entered the hold. The trickle became a stream and the stream a flood. The ship began to settle.

When the news was brought to the captain, he made the only possible decision. The ship must be abandoned. As the boats were lowered, the crewman who had been assigned to feed and care for Moifaa turned to the captain.

"What about him, sir?" he said, pointing to the stall which could barely be seen across the storm-shrouded deck.

"There's nothing to be done," replied the captain. "We can't reach him, and we can't carry him. He'll have to go down."

With that they cast off the lines and turned the tiny boat away from the sinking ship. But as they went, the haze lifted for a moment, and the seaman caught a final glimpse of the stall. What he saw made him cry out. "He's breaking loose. I can see his head." Then the storm closed in again, and the men in the lifeboat were alone upon the angry sea.

And indeed Moifaa too was abandoning ship. He did not, of course, understand the storm or the actions of the crew or the condition of the sinking steamer; but he did sense danger. Water swirled about his legs and the deck tilted dangerously. He knew he could not remain where he was. With a twist of his powerful neck he snapped the restraining ropes. Almost at the same time his hoofs crashed against the stall gate. It broke open, and the horse, caught in a giant wave, was swept across the slanted deck. The rail loomed before him. Gathering his strength, he leaped over it and plunged into the boiling sea.

In London, news of the disaster was brought to Spencer Gollans. He was Moifaa's owner and a well-known New Zealand horse breeder. For several years Gollans had been training his horse as a steeplechaser in order that he might be entered in England's famed Grand National steeplechase. Moifaa had won race after race in Australia and New Zealand, and Gollans had ordered him shipped to England so that he might try to add the world's most famous jumping event to his list of victories. But now it appeared that all this work and expense would be for naught. No horse from New Zealand would run in the 1904 Grand National.

But Gollans underestimated the strength and courage of his horse. Moifaa was not one to give up easily, on the race track or in the midst of a raging storm. True, when the animal plunged into the ocean he was confused and frightened. He thought only of escaping from the ship and the noise of the wind and thunder. But once he was afloat, he became more calm. His great belly bore him up well, and his strong legs carried him forward as easily as oars. The water was rough and cold but far less unpleasant than the narrow stall had been. Since the horse knew nothing of distance or geography, he was not overwhelmed, as a man might be, by the thought of being hundreds of miles from land. He was only out for a swim, as he had been many times before in New Zealand.

The night passed and still Moifaa swam on. In the darkness he passed without recognition a few bits of wood, clothing and the remains of a capsized boat. The steamer's crew would not come home again. The only survivor of this shipwreck was a horse.

Toward morning the storm subsided, and with the dawn there came a pleasant surprise. A long narrow strip of land lay across the horizon. Moifaa was tiring now, but he could smell grass and see trees. He pressed forward. Within an hour his hoofs touched a soft sand bottom. The weary horse stumbled up a gentle beach onto a small island. There was salt grass to eat and brackish water to drink. He had survived, and now he rested.

For weeks the horse lived on that island with no companions other than the seabirds which came and went about the beach. He was not really lonely in the sense that humans can be lonely. Perhaps he missed his companions from the ranch in New Zealand. Certainly, he did not miss the ship or its crew. What mattered was that he had food and drink and a place to run. That was enough.

Moifaa might well have lived out his life on that island were it not for Bent Zuidel's water keg. Zuidel was a fisherman, and he regularly sailed the waters off his home at Cape Town. He knew all the islands in the area, including the one where Moifaa was living, but he had no reason to visit them. His interest was in what might be found in the water not on the deserted dots of land. But one day as he fished along the coast, Zuidel accidentally knocked his precious keg of water overboard. It was a long and thirsty trip home, so he decided to land on the nearest island to get a bucket of spring water.

As he came ashore, Bent was startled to see a horse trotting toward him along the beach. He was a large animal, and the way he moved marked him as a thoroughbred. What, he thought, could a horse like this be doing on a tiny island? Then suddenly he remembered. He had read in the newspapers of the terrible shipwreck and the loss of the famous horse that was being shipped to England for the Grand National. This must be Moifaa, the great racer! Somehow he had survived. Hardly pausing to fill his water bucket, the fisherman jumped back into his small boat and headed for port.

From Cape Town a telegram was dispatched to Gollans in London. Upon reading the description of the marooned animal, he knew at once that it was Moifaa. The message he sent back was short but clear: SEND THE HORSE TO LONDON. SPARE NO EXPENSE. WASTE NO TIME. Within hours a large boat was on its way to the island. The horse was put aboard and transported to Cape Town, where a larger steamer awaited him. Safe on board and in a much larger stall, Moifaa was borne away to England.

Spencer Gollans stood on the dock at Liverpool harbor as the ship from South Africa tied up. With him was his trainer, Owen Hickey. They watched as their horse was lowered in a sling hung from the vessel's side. The sight that greeted their eyes was not a happy one. Moifaa was thin and unkempt. He had eaten nothing but salt grass for over a month and then, though well fed, had spent another three weeks in cramped quarters aboard ship. He was out of shape and had gone without the care of an experienced groom for months. The two men looked at each other. Finally Hickey spoke. "It's only a week till the race. I don't know if we can do it."

"If we can, he can," responded Gollans. "Let's get on with it."

In truth, though his words belied it, Gollans knew that they had little going for them but faith. But that had sustained him before. In some ways the New Zealander was quite different from the owners of the other horses entered in the Grand National. He was not an aristocrat but rather more like a rough-cut cowpoke from the American West. He was born poor and started his career as a stable boy. He knew and loved horses as only one who has curried and fed and tended them in time of illness can. And Moifaa was his greatest achievement. He had been present at the gelding's birth, and he had watched him grow and develop. He loved the horse almost as a child, and he had mourned his presumed loss as he might that of a family member. Now that the animal had so remarkably returned, he felt that some strange force was driving them both to a momentous and fateful climax. He would give his all to be ready for that moment.

Owen Hickey, Gollans's trainer, was equally moved by the situation. He had trained Moifaa and had seen him develop into the greatest racer New Zealand had ever produced. He knew only too well how little regard the fine English gentlemen and their snobbish trainers had for the "down under" upstarts and their champion. He longed to prove that his horse could meet the challenge. Yet, he doubted the possibility. The task seemed too great for even a horse of this caliber. Perhaps, he thought, they should have waited. Next year Moifaa would be in better shape. But one look at Gollans's set face ended any thought of that. They would race now, and it would be his job to bring the gelding to a winning peak. He patted the great horse's flank once more and led him away from the dock.

Aintree, where the Grand National is held, is not far from Liverpool, in the area of England known as Lancashire. Moifaa was loaded into a horse van and taken there. He was stabled with the other twenty-nine horses entered in the race, but he bore little resemblance to them. Most had been at Aintree for several weeks preparing for the race, and all had been over the course several times and were thoroughly familiar with it. They were sleek and well fed, trained to a fine point for what would be the most important race of their careers. Moifaa was underweight and out of shape, and there would be little time to remedy this. Moreover, he had not been on a race track for over six months.

Still there was hope. This horse from New Zealand was no ordinary nag. Dark brown in color, he was strongly muscled and larger than most steeplechasers. His hindquarters were unusually well developed, and he could spring over a five-foot fence with no more effort than a man might use in crossing a curb. Nor was strength the gelding's only attribute. He was highly intelligent for his kind, with an unusual ability to pick his way through the smallest openings in a crowded field of horses. When one adds to this the great endurance which had stood him in such good stead on the island, one understands the high hopes his owner and trainer had for Moifaa.

He had swept every race at home with a combination of speed and sure jumping. And, most important, he was that rare thing, a natural jumper. No one had to coax or teach him to jump. He loved the excitement and the challenge and had never been known to refuse or turn away from a hurdle. Given the length and difficulty of the course at Aintree, this characteristic could well prove critical.

Built in 1829, the Aintree race course has been the home of the Grand National since 1837. It is four and a half miles long and consists of a winding track, up and down hill, over no less than thirty jumps, each of which is different from all the others. Some are situated at the crest of hills, making it almost impossible for a horse to approach them at full speed. Others consist of a combination of jump and water hazard, while others are composed of several closely set walls or fences. Falls at the jumps are commonplace, and dozens of horses and more than one rider have died of injuries suffered in these terrible pile-ups. To win, even to finish, a horse must not only be fast and a good jumper but must also have extraordinary stamina and great courage. No one who had seen him run doubted Moifaa's courage and jumping ability; but would he, in his present condition, possess sufficient speed and stamina?

After all, the steeplechase is really a very simple race. The time in which a horse completes the course is unimportant. Form in jumping is unimportant. All that matters is who gets to the finish line first. There was little doubt that Moifaa could navigate any of the jumps. But could he get through all of them fast enough to defeat his rivals? This was the problem facing Gollans, Hickey and Arthur Birch, the man who was to make the ride.

Hickey was for feeding and conditioning. Build up the horse and keep him off the course so that he would not be injured in practice. Though he respected his trainer's knowledge, Gollans did not agree. Their entry was already too far behind the others in conditioning. They would have to take chances. "Moifaa loves to run and jump. He hasn't had a chance in months. Let's let him do it. Let him go over the course every day until he's dead beat, until he knows it like his own stable, until he owns it. If he falls, he falls. If he doesn't, then perhaps we'll see something."

And so they started. Other trainers and jockeys were awakened by the hoofbeats of the great gelding in the half light of dawn. They were disturbed at their evening meal by his return in the dusk. They became uneasy. After all, the horse did not gain weight. He became, if anything, even more gaunt. But every day he worked over the course. Other owners kept their horses' circuits of the track to a minimum to avoid injury, yet Moifaa and his masters seemed to relish the risk. True, he did not go very fast, but he did not fall. He would be there at the finish. That was something to think of.

Moreover, the horse had developed a following. He was already a legend, of course, for everyone in England knew of the shipwreck and his remarkable rescue. It would only be poetic justice for him now to triumph at Aintree, however unlikely that might seem to those who knew the odds he faced. But odds mean nothing to romantics; and as the days passed, more and more people, from street urchins to bankers, came to Aintree to watch him work out. As the day of the race approached, the crowds grew into hundreds.

The night before the race, as Moifaa rested in his stall, Gollans spoke to Birch. "We have done our best now. Unless another horse hits him, he will not fall. The others know this, and they fear him for it. Since they do not know yet how fast he can go, they will have to go faster and some will fall. If enough fall, we will have a chance."

As they talked, a steady rain drenched the countryside, and by dawn the course was soft and muddy. The bright flags and bunting about the pavilion hung limp against a brooding gray sky. It was a bad day for a steeplechase. The ground was soft, and there would be accidents.

But despite the weather the stands were packed. Drawn by the presence of the remarkable horse who had returned from the sea to race again, the largest crowd in Grand National history filled the seats, the space before the pavilion and the grassy areas alongside the finish line.

When Moifaa paraded to the starting line, a great roar went up from the assembled throng. It was easy to see which horse was the sentimental favorite. But those who fancied they knew horses had other favorites. The odds against Moifaa were twenty to one. He was a distinct underdog.

This, however, was of no concern to Gollans. To be the bettors' favorite was unimportant. What counted was to be the winner. His instructions to Birch were short but firm: "Stay in the pack till the halfway point; then, when the field spreads out, let him go. If he can, he'll run them all down for you."

Moifaa, of course, understood nothing of all this. He only knew that once again he was about to race. The smell of the other horses and the sound of the track were all about him. His blood raced with the desire to be away, to be doing what he liked better than anything else. He hungered to run, to jump and, most of all, to push ahead of those others. He had always hated the sight of another horse before him on the track.

At the starter's gun, the field broke away and headed for the first jump. Moifaa wanted to go immediately to the lead, but Birch restrained him, even though the favorites quickly put several lengths of daylight between themselves and the rest of the pack. There would be time enough to deal with them later. Now Moifaa hung back, moving easily across the uneven ground. Everyone cleared the first and second fences with no difficulty, but at the third, a high wall atop a hill, several horses went down in a pile and others turned away to avoid the accident. As his trainers had planned, Moifaa was far enough back to avoid the jumble and was able to pick his way through and cross the wall with little loss of time.

The horse was now into his familiar pattern. His muscles were liked coiled iron springs. His tail stood out like a banner. Jump after jump loomed before him. Jump after jump he cleared. The field began to string out; some horses laboring now, others still moving easily. The two leaders were only about ten lengths ahead of Moifaa's group.

About midway through the course they approached the notorious Canal Turn, a high brush barrier backed by a pool of water. The animal directly in front of Moifaa suddenly halted, refusing to jump and catapulting his rider over his head. Birch swung sharply right to avoid the fallen man, while a third horse, coming out of nowhere, crashed headlong into the riderless one. More horses were coming in now, and the area before the fence was filling up with horses and riders. There was no room to maneuver and no time to lose. Birch dug his spurs into Moifaa's sides and shouted in his ear. The horse knew what was expected. From a standing start less than twelve feet from the barrier, he sprang straight up and over, splashing into the pool beyond.

Now the gelding was third, but he had lost precious moments. The leaders were far ahead, waging their private battle for supremacy. But they reckoned without the great gelding. The hour appointed was at hand. Birch leaned forward in his saddle and put the crop to Moifaa's side. Only once, that was enough. The horse sprang forward as though from a catapult. He knew now that he could run, and his only thought was to overtake the two horses ahead of him.

Moifaa flew over the course, his mane flattened in the wind, his hoofs striking fire from the rocky soil. Foot by foot he gained. Spectators at the far end of the course saw him coming on, and the word spread like wildfire. The great New Zealand horse was now third and going after the leaders. Could he do it? Could the miracle really happen?

The crucial test occurred at Becher's Brook. A high double-rail fence with a wide ditch on the landing side, it was named for a Captain Becher, who fell there in 1839 after having won the first two Grand Nationals. High and difficult to approach, the jump was a severe test for any horse, particularly one tired after a long run. And it is true that Moifaa was beginning to tire now, though his competitive spirit burned as brightly as ever. He still pursued the front runners, though they, running neck and neck, were not even aware of his presence until they came down the hill to Becher's.

Suddenly, as though out of the blue, another horse appeared. It was the gelding. He had overtaken them. The three animals went at the jump as one, rising, then falling as they cleared it. But only two went on thereafter. A great bay, exhausted and unsteady, had gone down in the ditch. He struggled valiantly to his feet, but his hope of victory was now gone. Moifaa and a black stallion were left alone to contest the lead.

The crowd was now jammed about the finish line. They could see the horses, a half mile away, turning into the last lap. They were still side by side, and it looked like they would remain that way until the end. But such was not to be the case. Birch rose in his saddle. He dug his spurs into Moifaa's flanks and called for the last effort. The horse responded gladly. His mighty stride lengthened, and he began to move inexorably ahead. Wider and wider grew the lead as the crowd gasped. The gelding seemed almost to fly over the ground as he drew away from his beaten opponent. A length, two lengths, four, eight—the New Zealander thundered across the finish line the winner by eight full lengths. The impossible dream had come true!

Death of the King

Lobo was now trapped in the box canyon. Before him were three great wolfhounds, behind him a sheer rock wall hundreds of feet high. But his predicament came as no surprise. After all, he knew this canyon as he did all the country for miles about. His choice of route had been a deliberate one—intended to split the pack of pursuing hounds and thus assure the escape of his band and his beloved mate, Blanca.

So now he faced the dogs. They came at the wolf with a rush, racing to be the first to sink teeth into the hated outlaw. But Lobo was not easy meat. Big, indeed huge, for a gray wolf, he stood three feet at the shoulder and weighed over one hundred and fifty pounds. His teeth, honed on the bones of fallen steers, were like rapiers, and his muscles were spring steel.

The first to attack was Juno, the pack's lead dog. Nearly as large as Lobo and fully as fierce, she struck like a whirlwind. Shoulder to shoulder they fought, seeking an opening for tooth or claw. And it came, as is so often the case, by cruel chance. Recovering from a lunge at her foe, Juno slipped on loose gravel and rolled on her side. Lobo was on her in a flash, his great teeth tearing at her soft underbelly. Twisting in agony as she was torn apart, the hound took a measure of vengeance.

Her own jaws closed on Lobo's haunch, and even as her life drained away she tore a great patch of flesh from him.

And now the other dogs came on slavering with rage. Neither was as large as the fallen leader but both were brave and they were two. For a long time they fought Lobo in the canyon's shadow, but again his strength and experience prevailed. He crushed the head of one hound and left the other to crawl back home with a maimed leg. The fight was over. After a few minutes to rest and lick his bleeding wounds, the wolf slowly climbed out of the canyon and set about the task of gathering his scattered band.

For all of his life Lobo had lived in the valley of the Corrumpaw River in northern New Mexico, and for all of his life it had been like this: fighting, killing, running from men and dogs. Once it must have been different—before the cattle- and sheepmen came, when the range was open and the wolves matched wits and strength only with their natural prey, the fleet antelope and the dangerous bison. But now, like all things which refused to be tamed, the wolves were forced farther and farther into the waste places, the narrow gorges and dry hills shunned by men.

But there was no food in those lonely spots. The bison and nearly all the antelope were gone, slain by the newcomers. So the wolves turned to what was at hand, the fat cattle and sheep which grazed in the lush green valleys. And for this men called them killers and hunted them without mercy.

Once he had reached the top of the nearby mesa, Lobo halted. He sniffed the air slowly, delicately, as though savoring a fine meal; then, raising his head, he called. The long rumbling wolf howl carried far across the broken land, and from a distance it was answered. First one voice, then another took up the chorus. One, two, three, four. Yes, all his band had escaped the hunters.

Now the great wolf moved more quickly. Breaking into a trot, he turned north into the headwaters of the Corrumpaw. Here the land was even more twisted, with narrow dry watercourses thick with cactus and prickly pear. In one of these the

Death of the King

206

band had their lair. No trail led there, for the way, chosen for safety, passed over bare rock. Only instinct and a keen nose showed the way. Lobo passed unerringly through dozens of similar gullies until he came at dusk to his own home. His four companions awaited him.

Blanca, his mate of several summers, nuzzled his wounds. Her concern was evident in the nervous way she paced the dirt floor of the shallow cave in which the band slept. Amarillo, the yellow one, sat apart as he usually did. He did not come forward like the others to greet the leader. This caused Lobo no concern. He did not value Amarillo's companionship. It was his speed of foot that was important. More than once when the band was desperate with hunger and the sheepfolds and cattle pens were closed against them, the yellow wolf had run an antelope to ground and shared it with his companions. He did his job. That was enough.

The two other members of the pack were more sociable. Younger and light tan in hue, they were as alike as twins. The offspring of Lobo and Blanca's first mating some three seasons ago, they had now reached full maturity and full membership in the clan.

Lobo gazed at his offspring fondly. He and Blanca had had three litters. Some of the children had died, most had gone off to make their own lives in the dangerous hills. These two, brother and sister, had chosen to remain. Wolves, in common with most wild animals, have little interest in their children beyond the cub stage. But Lobo and his mate were not quite typical in this regard. True, they defended their prerogatives against all comers including the twins, but there was also a deep affection shown among the family members.

This closeness grew, no doubt in part from the parents' own relationship. Unlike many of their fellows, they remained together throughout the year, not merely meeting at mating time; and there was a closeness between them that would have done justice to a human couple. This affection could be seen in its obvious physical manifestations—nuzzling, lying closely together and so on—but it was manifested on another plane as well. Lobo and Blanca seemed at times to be able to read each other's thoughts and to respond when needed though miles apart. On more than one occasion this had stood them in good stead.

As darkness enveloped the cave, the five animals sat quietly resting and waiting. In a few hours the moon would be up, and it would be time to hunt.

Miles away, where the Corrumpaw ran wide and slow between green fields of tall grass, Tannery the hunter waited for his wolfhounds. What he saw did not please him. Only a few dogs came back, and these were footsore and crippled from fighting. The man swore as he saw them limp into the ranch yard. He was a Texas Ranger and he had hunted men as well as beasts, but never before had a foe taken such a toll.

"That Lobo is a devil, not a wolf," he snarled to the rancher at his side.

"No, he's a wolf, right enough," replied Joe Calone. "He and his band have been around here for over four years, since 'eighty-nine at least, and we figure that they've cost us a heifer or a calf a day. That's over two thousand head by now, to say nothing of the sheep and dogs they rip up just for fun. They're just plain killers, that's all."

And certainly to ranchers like Joe Calone, who had once lost two hundred sheep to the wolves in a single night, or professional hunters like Art Tannery, whose hounds Lobo had destroyed, they were killers—the most fearsome plague the Corrumpaw country had seen since the last of the Indians had been driven off. True, despite the many rumors and legends current among whites and Indians alike, wolves will not normally attack a man unless cornered or hurt, still their legendary skill and ruthlessness have caused them to be a source of terror to the plains dwellers. For, after all, how could beasts which could slaughter a young calf or full-grown ewe not be dangerous to man? For such creatures extermination was the only answer.

But to the wolves it was just a matter of survival, and survival among great risks. The moon was still low on the horizon when Lobo's band came forth. Traveling single file and staying in the shadows, they passed quietly and quickly down the upper gorge until they came to the grasslands. A mist hung over the river, and along its banks large groups of cattle stood or lay. All seemed quiet, but the air held a scent of danger. There were men about, and Lobo's keen nose had detected them. He growled low in his throat and turned away. Reluctantly the others followed. Men meant guns, and some way, by instinct or experience, Lobo knew that to face an armed man meant certain death. There would be no beef tonight, but they would eat.

Again the great wolf led the way, this time up away from the river and into the low scrub-covered hills. Here grass was sparse —poor forage for a cow but quite enough to sustain sheep, and sheep were quite enough to sustain wolves.

About a mile from the river there was a crude sheepfold constructed of stone and wood, and within it were several dozen animals. Leaving his companions concealed in the shadows, Lobo circled the enclosure, looking for a weak spot. The sheep smelled him and grew restless, but there was no barking and no man smell. This bunch had been deemed too few to warrant a guard in a country where tens of thousands of their fellows roamed the hills; still there was the pen with its high walls topped by barbed wire. It could not be broken into, but there was another way.

Lobo returned to his band. He gave no sign discernible to man, but they knew that it was time to eat. The wolves followed him silently to the enclosure. Then, in a single leap, Lobo cleared six feet of stone and wire and fell like a thunderbolt among the frightened, bleating sheep. He seized one in his jaws and turned and sprang out again. Four more times he repeated his trip.

Early the next day the rancher came to open his fold. The animals within appeared to be well, and they were released for the day's feeding. Their number did seem oddly diminished, though. The rancher wished he could remember just how many there had been in that particular pen. In a hollow just a few hundred feet away, carrion birds were picking the bones of five sheep the rancher would never miss, while back in their lair the wolf band slept the sleep of the well fed.

And so it went for many months, with the courage and sagacity of Lobo's band matched against the wiles of the hunters and stockmen. As the wolves' depredations grew, so did their reputations, until there was not a rancher in all New Mexico who did not know of Lobo and curse his name. But, of course, fame does have its disadvantages. More than one man saw in the killing of the great wolf the possibility of fame and fortune, and so the little band became the center of much unwelcome attention.

Hunters loosed their dogs against them, only to see the animals swallowed up in the twisting canyons and trackless wastes of the high country. Still hunters waited for days over a carcass hoping for a shot at the elusive killers, but they did not come. Little did the men know that Lobo's band were not scavengers. They ate only what they killed.

Poisons and traps were tried, of course, but the ranchers who set them were inexperienced, and the wolves had little trouble detecting their danger. But others were not so fortunate, and dozens of coyotes, jack rabbits and ground squirrels died in those traps to which the wolf band seemed immune.

So, though his enemies detected no sign of relaxation in his vigilance, Lobo might, indeed, have come to feel that he was invincible. At times he did display what in a man would have been termed bravado. Like during the summer of 1891 when he and Blanca raised their cubs in a cave no more than a thousand feet from Joe Calone's ranch house. It was a thousand feet straight up, of course, on a narrow ledge inaccessible to dogs or humans. Joe found them out, however, and having suffered so much because of Lobo, he determined to have his revenge. He tried just about everything. He sat below with his rifle, ready to fire at anything that moved. Nothing moved. He covered the trail to the ledge with traps and poisoned meat. The traps were harmlessly sprung, the meat lay untouched. Finally he even resorted to lowering sticks of dynamite down the cliff. He never could get the fuse length right, however, and all he ever managed to do was dump a lot of rock and dirt on his own roof.

Things really couldn't go on like that. Late in 1893 the ranchers put a price of a thousand dollars on Lobo's head and turned the job over to professional killers. Lobo saw them come. From a vantage point high on a bluff he watched the men slowly work their way across the plains. They were sowing the land with traps and poison. More than one innocent calf died so that its carcass might be laced with strychnine. Others were cut to pieces for trap bait—traps which were cunningly placed beneath the surface of the ground, there to lie in wait for some beast's unsuspecting step.

The war had begun in earnest. Now when Lobo led his companions out each night, he went with every sense alert for the unnatural smell or shape that could spell danger. And he found danger. A familiar path to the water hole took on an unfamiliar appearance. Though the difference was slight, it was enough to tell Lobo that here lay a trap, a huge bear trap buried right next to the clear water. The wolf scratched it out, sprung it, perhaps to show his disdain, then led his companions on to the spring.

But the task seemed endless. Every day the traps were more complex. Lobo sensed that he was fighting against a powerful and diabolical mind. The sheepfolds and cattle pens were ringed with traps, the trails festooned with them. The water holes were poisoned. Yet, the wolves survived. Lobo broke into the cattle pens, waylaid the stray sheep and found new springs. He picked a way through the traps. He eluded the snares and pitfalls. The hunters cursed, for the wolves seemed to live charmed lives.

But Lobo was troubled. For himself he had no fear, nor for his band if they obeyed and followed him. His nose and his instinct were foolproof. But alone or out of his control the others were in great danger. For Blanca he was particularly concerned. She had a wild streak, an unpredictable disposition —something which he had always loved but now had come to fear. She was too curious, too forgetful of what he had taught. On more than one occasion he had had to call her back when she had broken from the pack. Too often what had drawn her away proved to be a well-concealed trap or a cunningly poisoned bait.

Unfortunately, this characteristic had been observed by others. The master hunter, on his daily trips to the empty traps, had noticed the small track which often strayed from that of the other wolves. When he learned that Lobo had a mate, he quickly guessed that it was she. No male would have been allowed such leeway. The mind of man, so cruel and calculating compared with that of even the most vicious beast, began to work. A plan was devised.

There came a gray morning in February when Lobo's pack encountered yet another dead calf, like all the others poisoned and circled by traps. Though the traps were, as always, cleverly placed, the ground swept clean and no smell of man left, Lobo recognized the danger immediately. Yet he could not pass it by. Like all wolves, he had a dangerous weakness. Those of his breed could never resist the temptation to examine carrion even though they had no intention of eating it.

As he had done many times before, the great wolf warily circled the body, finding and exposing each of the deadly traps. His companions cautiously followed in his footsteps. All but one. Blanca had seen something else. Some distance from the calf lay its head, cruelly severed and seemingly cast aside. Now, wolves will not eat heads except when starving, so it was only fatal curiosity that drew her to the spot. Still, she came as the hunter knew she would, and it was her undoing. Before Lobo could call her away or reach her, Blanca had fallen into the fatal trap, a huge steel vise which gripped her forelegs without compassion or hope of release.

Lobo knew traps and knew that there could be no escape. He sent the others back to safety and sat with Blanca through the night.

Dawn brought the hunter, and with him came death. Lobo withdrew to the hills, for he knew that he could not face the guns, and Blanca was strangled with lariats and dragged away to the ranch house. That night the hunter lay in his bed and listened to the sound of Lobo's wailing. The wolf had followed the trail of his dead companion into the very heart of enemy territory, and now he prowled the darkness outside the cabin mourning his loss. Those who heard him shuddered, for never had they heard so sad a lament. But none ventured outside, for in the darkness a rifle would have been of little use. Toward morning the cries died away; and the hunter smiled a smile worthy of any wolf as he contemplated the next step in his plan.

Soon after the sun rose, Blanca's carcass was brought from the shed where it had lain during the night and was dragged away into the hills. Other bodies lay about the ranch house, those of the watchdogs which had foolishly disturbed Lobo at his mourning, but these were left behind. Blanca was what was needed.

At the foot of the very canyon where she had lived so long with her mate, Blanca was laid out as though for some grisly wake, her body embraced by dozens of traps and her scent laid thick on the surrounding ground and bushes. The work was done before noon, and the men returned home to wait.

The day passed. Carrion birds circled overhead. Curious rabbits surveyed the scene. But nothing stirred in the canyon. Then, when the sun had set, Lobo came, moving heavily along the trail as though he bore a great burden. He went straight to the body. He did not need to search for it. All day his nose had been telling him what lay at the mouth of the valley.

Lobo went to Blanca, straight through the traps. As they closed on his legs he tore them from their moorings and dragged them after him, even the largest, the bear traps anchored to six-foot logs. When he reached his dead mate, he was dragging hundreds of pounds of wood and steel. He lay down against her cold body and closed his eyes.

The next morning the hunter rose with the sun. It was barely light when he raced his horse down into the gully mouth. His hopes were realized. There lay Lobo. At the sight of his tormentor, the wolf's lethargy fell away. He rose and sprang at the horse. But his burden was too great. He sank back helpless. The men approached. One poked a rifle in the beast's face. The great jaws closed on the barrel. A lasso floated through the air. Lobo cut it in two before it could settle about his neck.

The men stared in awe at their foe, so terrible even in this extremity. Some wished to kill him then and be done with it, but the hunter had other ideas. He wanted his triumph to be complete. He wanted the wolf alive. More ropes were brought, and with a log between his teeth and his legs bound, Lobo was borne away to the ranch. There he was chained to a wall to await the promised spectacle. Tomorrow, all the ranchers in the valley would be coming to see and mock their fallen enemy.

But Lobo was strangely silent. He did not struggle or try to attack the jeering men who crowded about him. In fact, he seemed to take no notice of his captors. His eyes were fixed on the distant hills of his domain, and he neither moved nor gave tongue. He was certainly not the object of fun the cowboys had anticipated; but perhaps tomorrow when a crowd gathered, things would be different. The men drifted off to bed.

The following day the first visitors to the corral found the wolf as he had been left, head on his paws, eyes gazing at the far boundaries of his empire. But the eyes were lifeless. Lobo, king of the Corrumpaw, had gone home.

A Rabbit with
Nine Lives

John White took a long drink from his coffee cup and put it back down on the edge of the conveyor frame. The mug jiggled softly in time to the vibration of the moving belt. He shivered slightly as he looked about the bleak factory. Grit and pieces of broken cinder block were everywhere. The air was thick with dust; and it was cold, had been cold for two days now—the kind of English damp that goes into your bones. Coffee tasted good on a day like this. He reached for the cup again.

As he picked up his coffee, White's gaze wandered idly up the long conveyor belt. Its broad tan surface was dotted with gray building blocks. Like an army of infinite numbers they poured out of the huge stamping machine in the far wall and marched slowly past him on their way to the sorting tables. John really had nothing much to do with these blocks. His job was to see that the belt functioned properly—eight hours a day just watching it go by. What a way to earn a living. And, of course, nothing really ever happened to break the monotony.

But then something did happen. White's eye was drawn to one of the cinder blocks. It was misbehaving. It was not jiggling contentedly along with its companions. It was moving about in an odd manner, almost hopping; and its actions had nothing to do with the customary vibrations of the belt. What was going on here?

White rose from his seat and peered closely at the passing block. As he watched, a crack appeared in its damp surface. It was as though something were trying to get out. In spite of himself, the man started back. There could be nothing in that cinder block. But there was!

The block cracked open like an eggshell, and a tiny head emerged. Fascinated beyond belief, the man followed the chunk of concrete as it moved down the line. What in the world did it contain? And then he saw. With a last effort which split its cement prison, an animal forced itself free and stood up. It was a young brown rabbit less than a foot long.

John gently lifted the bedraggled creature from the belt and carried it to a nearby sink. The rabbit's fur was matted and covered with drying cement, but his eyes were bright; and even in John's hands it fought for freedom. The man washed him gently beneath the tap and then swaddled him in a towel. Soon the rabbit was resting quietly before an electric heater while a crowd of workers stared at him and speculated on how he could have survived his remarkable and terrifying journey.

For the rabbit, that journey had started in a most innocent manner. He had been asleep. Daylight had come late to the burrow that day, for the thick clouds that hung over the countryside had prolonged the night. It was well after eight when the mother roused herself. The sudden removal of warmth awakened the young one. He flailed about for a moment, disentangling himself, and then became instantly aware of hunger. It seemed that he was always hungry now that his mother had ceased to nurse him. Why that had occurred he did not know. He understood only that eating was a lot more trouble than it was before—though it was more exciting. The thought of woods and field, the sights, sounds and smells of the feeding grounds came to the rabbit. He hopped out of the hole.

The small animal passed silently and almost invisibly through the thin woods. His soft brown fur tinged with darker guard hairs blended perfectly into the dun-colored winter vegetation, and his soft pads left little mark on the forest floor. Yet the rabbit was constantly on the alert. His dark nose twitched continually as he searched the air for the smell of dogs, foxes or the myriad other enemies which he had learned at such an early age to fear; and the faint white bands about his brown eyes gave him a constant look of strained apprehension. It took time to find a meal, and the small one knew only too well that as he hunted, others hunted him.

An hour or so had passed when the rabbit reached the sand pit. He had never seen anything like it. To him it must have seemed like a great desert, a seemingly endless expanse of brown waste stretching away on all sides. He sensed that there would be nothing to eat here; still, it was strange and therefore enticing. He started across.

Robert McQuillen slid the pile of orders across his desk and picked up the telephone. He hadn't expected things to be so busy this time of year. There must be a lot of building going on in London. Well, the more work the better. Times were hard, and he didn't want to lay off any men.

The man who answered McQuillen's call had been waiting for it all morning in a small shack at the edge of the sand pit. His name was Richard Bennett, and he ran the giant mechanical scoop which dug sand for the Axminster Brick Works.

When he picked up the phone, Bennett heard McQuillen's familiar voice. "Hello, Bennett, this is the office. We are going to need more sand this morning. I want to work the stamping machine all day."

"Yes, sir," Bennett replied. He put down the telephone and went out to the scoop. Taller than a three-story building, the great apparatus hung over the pit. Its huge mechanical maw could swallow yards of sand in a single gulp.

After climbing into the cab, the worker activated the scoop. A low roar came from somewhere within it, and as gears were shifted, the great arm swung slowly out over the pit.

The rabbit was about halfway across the sand when he heard the sound of an engine. Living close to the pit, he had heard similar sounds before but never so close. He was frightened. For a moment he crouched undecided. In the woods he would have fled to a hole or a thicket, but here everything looked the same. A monstrous shadow passed over him, and he turned to run.

At that moment the hungry jaws of the sand scoop bit into the hillside below him. Suddenly, he felt the ground beneath his feet tilting upward. He was sliding down, sinking into a soft sea of loose sand. Terrified, the animal gathered himself to leap clear. As he sprang upward, the lip of the scoop came free of the ground. The rabbit crashed into a wall of iron and fell back on top, fortunately for him, of thirty tons of sand.

Bennett swung the controls and brought the scoop clear of the sand quarry. Along the edge of the pit stood a line of metal hoppers each one large enough to hold a single bucket of sand. He poised the bucket over the nearest of these and reached for the release button. In an instant the stunned rabbit would be buried beneath tons of sand. Just then the noon whistle blew. It was lunchtime. Leaving the scoop where it hung, the worker went off to eat.

The rabbit became aware of things again. He was lying on his back almost buried in sand. He didn't understand how he had gotten where he was, but he didn't intend to stay there. It took the animal only a few minutes to determine that he was trapped. All around him reared high steel walls. Only one side presented the hope of escape. The bucket had been left in a tilted position, and at a single point an incline existed.

The trapped animal did the only thing he knew how to do. He leaped as far as he could up the steep steel wall. But the metal was slick, and his blunt nails found no grip. He slid back into the sand. Again and again the rabbit tried, to no avail. At last a new idea occurred to him. Backing clear across the bucket, he came at the obstacle on the dead run. Up he went and over, his forelegs just grasping the edge of the bucket and propelling him forward. Down he fell, but not to freedom. He fell, instead, into the next hopper, which, fortunately, had been filled with sand the night before. He wasn't free, but at least when Bennett returned from lunch there was only sand to be dumped into the empty hopper.

Crouching in a shaded corner of the hopper, the rabbit waited to see what would happen next. He knew that he could not escape at the moment, for the new container had four tall and perfectly straight sides. He could only hope that some new opportunity to get away would present itself. But none did. What did happen was that after what seemed a terribly long time the hopper began to move. It was part of a conveyor system, and when Bennett pulled yet another switch the whole line of hoppers began to travel slowly away from the sand pit and toward the factory in the valley below.

Rocking and bumping, the hoppers swung across the valley hundreds of feet above the earth. The rabbit flattened himself against the shifting sands, seeking some stability in a world turned suddenly alien.

On the roof of the brick works stood a tall overhead mixer. It was here that the sand from the quarry was blended with cement and water and coal cinders to produce the proper composition for cinder blocks. As surely as time passes, the line of hoppers approached the mixer.

The first sign of danger was the rain. The rabbit had been rained on before but never like this. It seemed as though tons of water were pouring out of the sky upon him. And, worse yet, mixed with the liquid was a fine dust—dry cement—which covered him with a choking mist. Gasping and coughing, the soaked animal cowered in his prison. Within a few minutes the hopper was half flooded, and the rabbit was swimming for his life in a thick inedible porridge.

And worse was yet to come. The container began to vibrate, then to spin, slowly at first, then faster and faster. It had become a cement mixer!

It appeared that there was now little hope for the rabbit. As he was swirled about within the spinning bucket, the animal rose and fell beneath the surface of the cinder-block mix. He could barely breathe and could not see at all, for his eyes were filled with the gooey mixture. Suddenly, though, a remarkable thing happened. So great became the force of rotation that the little victim was flung up and completely out of the hopper. He hurtled through the air and fell soggily on the chain link belt which joined the line of containers.

For a long time he lay there on the hard steel. He was sick from the spinning motion and nearly exhausted, but he was still unwilling to give up. Slowly the rabbit dragged himself to a sitting position. He licked his paws until they were free of concrete, and then with them he cleaned out his eyes and ears. All the time he was doing this the buckets above him continued to turn.

At last, able to see and to hear again, the rabbit took stock of his situation. What he discovered could not have pleased him. He had landed on a band of iron barely three feet wide and two feet long. At each end of his perch there was a hopper. At each side there was nothing. The mixing tower was a great open shaft, and he was suspended in it, a hundred feet above the ground. There was, once more, no escape.

As he sat there contemplating this newest misfortune, the animal became aware of a change. It had grown quiet. The hoppers had stopped turning. The cinder-block mixture was now thoroughly mixed and ready to be made into blocks. The metal beneath the rabbit stirred again and came to life. The long line of containers began to move once more. The rabbit clung to the conveyor belt and felt himself borne slowly forward. Where was he going this time?

At the far side of the mixing tower there was a great door. Above the door there was a window, and in that window sat a man. For eight hours a day, six days a week, Andrew Rehn sat at his window watching the cement carriers come and go. It was his job to control the mixing of the cement, to open the door into the shaft which led down to the stamping machine, and to unload each hopper as it passed that door.

The conveyor belt made a U-turn right in front of the door, and as each bucket swung by, Rehn would pull a switch which caused it to tilt on its side and pour its load down into the shaft. It really wasn't hard work, but one had to pay attention to business, because if you pulled too soon or too late tons of cement would go splashing down the inside of the tower instead of into the stamper where they belonged. The boss didn't like that. It was like throwing money away.

Rehn peered through the window. One after another the containers rolled by. One after another he dropped their contents neatly down the black funnel. Only once did he falter. Just two cars from the end of the line he was distracted. He thought that he saw something on the belt between the hoppers. Was it moving? It almost looked like some sort of small animal. He pressed his face against the glass trying to get a better view, and he almost forgot to dump the oncoming bucket. He grabbed the lever and pulled frantically. Just in time! The hopper banged against the doorway, but nearly everything went down the shaft. That had been a close one. No more daydreaming for him. Still, he couldn't resist another glance up the line of now empty carriers. No, there was certainly nothing on the belt now. His eyes must really have been playing tricks on him.

The rabbit tried to maintain his balance on the swaying belt. Each time a pot was unloaded it would cause the whole line to lurch and vibrate. More than once he was nearly pitched off into space. But, though he did not know it, freedom was drawing near. Once the hoppers on each side of him were emptied, they would be turned around and headed out of the tower and back across the valley to the sand pit. When they and their tiny passenger got there, it would be an easy matter for him to hop down and get away into the woods.

Unfortunately, however, the rabbit never quite made it. Just as the bucket ahead of him reached the doorway, Rehn saw him and, in his surprise, was a little late in emptying it. The container banged against the door frame, the conveyor belt lurched, and the rabbit was knocked forward. Blackness loomed before him. He grabbed for something. There was nothing. He toppled headfirst down the inclined tunnel that led to the great stamping machine!

The rabbit was terrified. He could see nothing in the sudden blackness, and when he stopped falling he found that he was once more swimming for his life in a sea of liquid cement. And far worse awaited him, for that cement was moving steadily toward its final destination—a great stamping mold which compressed the cinder-block mixture into rectangular blocks some eighteen inches long.

The end came quite unexpectedly. The stream of concrete flowed over a slight drop down into a boxlike space. The rabbit sensed that he was trapped; and indeed he was, for the walls of the box were slowly closing about him. He was being compressed into a cinder block by a force of one hundred pounds per square inch.

But the machinery which was stamping out that block was programmed to produce only a thousand blocks. The rabbit was in block one thousand one. Obedient to its mechanical command, the stamper drew back. As mysteriously as it had come, the terrible pressure which had been crushing the rabbit ceased.

The sides of the mold drew back, and the incompletely compressed block rolled slowly out onto the conveyor belt. It was slightly larger than its fellows. It should have been, for in it was the rabbit, half dead from suffocation and fright but still miraculously alive. And even as his prison moved down the line toward John White's station, the courageous creature roused himself and began to fight again for his life. This time he would succeed.

Hidden Talents

Johnny hated doing homework, especially on nice days like this when the sun shone and there was sure to be a baseball game at the park. But the homework had to be done. The nine-year-old applied himself reluctantly to his math book while casting an envious glance at his dog, Chris, who was lying quietly by the desk. Boy! That Chris, all he ever had to do was eat, sleep and play. Johnny contemplated momentarily the attractiveness of being a dog, dismissing the idea only at the thought of dog food. Ugh! Still, dogs never had to do math. "Chris, you bum, wake up and tell me what seven and ten make," he said, prodding the dozing beagle with his foot.

Chris opened one eye and looked at his young master. It was a look of infinite boredom. The dog got slowly to his haunches, and then, as though he had been doing it all his life, he began to tap out a sum with his left paw. At first the boy watched this process with nothing more than amused tolerance. What new game had Chris invented now? Was he asking for a handout or just playing? Then something clicked in Johnny's mind. Just how many taps had that been? Could it be? He looked at his canine companion with new interest.

"Chris," Johnny said, very clearly and distinctly now, "how

much is two and two?" This time there could be no doubt about it. The answering taps totaled four! Johnny Anderson pulled his chair closer to the desk and went at his homework with a new enthusiasm. It looked like there was going to be time for that baseball game after all!

But, of course, secrets, especially good secrets, can seldom be kept long. Johnny's mother was understandably delighted with his sudden progress in mathematics but equally puzzled at how he achieved such fine results in such a short time. One afternoon she decided to look in on him. It was an idyllic scene, one to do any parent's heart good. There was Johnny at his desk, math book open before him and pencil poised. At his feet sat his faithful dog, Chris. Johnny was speaking to Chris. What was he saying? Mrs. Anderson drew nearer. Was he asking the dog sums? What was the dog doing? He seemed to be tapping his paw on the floor. Grace Anderson didn't understand this at all. She listened more closely. There was no doubt about it. Johnny was now asking the dog to add fourteen and twelve. Now the dog was again tapping the floor, and when he ceased, Johnny was writing something in his book.

Mrs. Anderson rushed into the room. She snatched up her son's math book and looked at the problems on the page. The last completed problem was the sum of fourteen and twelve. The answer was twenty-six. Grace Anderson looked at Johnny and she looked at Chris. Neither made a sound. They really didn't have to. She knew.

That night, instead of munching his bone beneath the kitchen sink or being relegated to the backyard, Chris joined the family in the big living room. Though he didn't know it, he was about to undergo the first of a long series of tests designed to determine the extent of his remarkable powers. Not having seen the dog in action, Robert Anderson was, to say the least, dubious about his wife's story. But one could not ignore Johnny's sudden and quite uncharacteristic improvement in the field of mathematics. He had suspected that the boy was getting help from someone, but from a dog? Well, he would have to see for himself.

Mr. Anderson looked down at Chris. "Chris," he said in a conversational tone, "go get my hat." The dog never budged. "See what I told you," he said, turning to his wife. "He can't understand English. How could he? He's only a dog."

"Ask him a sum, Dad," insisted his son. "Maybe that's all he knows. He never was much good at fetching."

"That's right," his father responded. "He's five years old and he can't even do tricks. All right, I'll give him one more try, though I think it's all pretty silly. Okay, Chris, what's ten and ten?"

At the sound of Anderson's voice the dog this time showed definite interest. He sat up and, as before, began to tap the floor with his paw. When he stopped, the total was twenty.

Well, it might just have been an accident, thought Mr. Anderson, though in his heart he had a terrible feeling that it wasn't. He tried a couple of more sums ending up with fifty and thirty and, naturally, losing count before the dog stopped tapping. But he'd had enough anyway. Robert Anderson was convinced, and he decided that someone who knew something more about animals had better hear about this.

And so the experts came: animal doctors, animal behaviorists, animal trainers, a whole host of people to marvel at Chris's unusual abilities. The dog seemed to enjoy all the testing, and it was not long before his questioners learned that he could do more than just add. He could also subtract, multiply and divide. He was practically a walking pocket calculator!

Johnny, of course, was at first delighted with all this—viewing Chris as a distinct hedge against the homework inflation which was bound to come with the fifth and sixth grades. It soon became evident, though, that things were not going to work out so well. His parents knew about Chris. His teachers found out. There were a few telephone calls, and Johnny soon found himself doing his homework without the assistance of man's best friend.

All the excitement, moreover, was affecting his relationship with Chris. After all, the animal was his pet, had been since he was a pup. They had slept in the same bed, roamed the streets and fields together, played tag in vacant lots. Now all of a sudden these people were hanging around, bothering Chris, checking him, asking him questions. Johnny felt left out. He hardly ever had a chance anymore to do the old fun things with Chris. It was like living with a movie star!

Not only that. Things just weren't simple anymore. Chris had been his confidant, the one being he could really trust. Now, he wasn't sure that he could tell the dog his secrets. After all, maybe there was a way that they could get that out of him too. Johnny still loved Chris, but for the first time he felt uneasy with him.

In the meantime, someone else found out something remarkable about Chris, and it wasn't one of the experts. Uncle Harry Ainsley had known the dog since he was a pup and had always treated the animal with great affection—petting him and bringing him soup bones to gnaw. When he heard of Chris's talents, it occurred to Harry that now perhaps the dog could do something for him.

Uncle Harry was a horse player and, like most, not a particularly successful one. Sure, he read all the dope sheets and knew all the handicappers; but somehow nearly every week he lost more than he won. Now, however, he saw a chance to reverse the process.

One afternoon Harry offered to take Chris for a walk. They didn't walk far, though, just over to Harry's house in the next block. There the experiment began. Even Harry felt that it was pretty crazy, and he was glad that there was no one else around to watch. But Harry was a desperate man, and if he succeeded . . .

Carefully placing on the floor an open newspaper listing the entrants for the day's races at a nearby track, Harry invited Chris to peruse it. The dog sniffed curiously at the paper and then lay down upon it. Hopeless, thought Harry. But he had to try. "Chris," he said, his voice choked with tension, "tell me which horse will win the first race." The dog looked puzzled. He nosed the paper. He whined. He clearly didn't understand.

Darned dog's no better at it than I am, thought Harry. At least he's got sense enough not to pick 'em. Maybe I'm going at it the wrong way. After all, just because he can add doesn't mean he can read. I bet that's it. I'll read him the entries. And that is what he did, carefully reciting the names of all the horses in the first race while Chris listened attentively. Then he asked the fatal question. Who will win? Without hesitation, the dog tapped his paw on the floor three times.

Uncle Harry carefully went through the whole eight-race program repeating the same process. Then he and the dog went for another walk. This one took them to a tiny candy store. It was an odd sort of store. Most of the candy under the dusty counter was pretty old, and one would have thought that the store didn't do much business. It did, though; but the business was all in the back room. There a man in a green eyeshade sat by a telephone taking bets. A half dozen horse players surrounded him, and the air was thick with horse talk and cigar smoke. The store was a bookie's headquarters.

Without hesitation, Harry put twenty dollars on each of Chris's choices for the eight races. Then he sat down to await the results. Chris, his job done, went to sleep.

The afternoon passed quickly. Outside it was a nice quiet afternoon. Inside it was turmoil. Uncle Harry had won the first two races without undue comment. When he won the third, including the first half of the daily double, people began to look at him oddly. By the time his fifth horse had come home a winner, the horse room was packed with spectators all wanting to see how far Harry could go. It was almost a foregone conclusion that Harry's sixth-race choice would be a winner, and it was; but when the seventh race came up, the tension really mounted. This was the second half of the daily double, and Uncle Harry, who had already made nearly a thousand dollars for the day, stood to collect three thousand more if his horse came in ahead.

Harry's face was beaded with perspiration. He was having trouble breathing. He wasn't a young man anymore, and the pressure was getting to him. The bookmaker wasn't feeling so good either. He had been taking the old man's money for years now, and suddenly it had all turned around. He hunched over the phone awaiting the fatal call. The phone rang. The bookie picked it up, listened for a moment, then turned to Harry. His face was ashen. Not a sound could be heard in the packed room. "You won," he said in a flat voice.

Harry Ainsley rose. He tried to speak. He clutched his heart, a bewildered look on his face, and then he slowly toppled forward. Felled by a heart attack at the moment of his greatest glory, Uncle Harry died there on the horse-room floor, and his secret knowledge died with him. No one else ever thought to ask Chris to pick a winner.

But, of course, people asked the remarkable dog a lot of other questions. And he also began answering, or so it seemed, when no problem was presented to him. He would simply begin to tap out series of numbers, ten, three, thirteen, and so on without any encouragement whatsoever. For a long time the investigators didn't know what to make of these random sounds; then, one day, Ronald Hitchings, a technician who was listening to a tape of them, realized with a start that all were in sequences of twenty-six or fewer taps. Of course, he reasoned, there are twenty-six letters in the alphabet, but that could be just a coincidence. If the dog could understand human language, perhaps he had also in some way learned to communicate in it.

Ronald Hitchings wasted no time. That very afternoon he

went to see Chris. The dog was reclining at his ease on the Anderson front porch, a badly mangled beef bone between his paws. Instead of the usual mathematical quiz, the man simply looked Chris in the eye and said, "How can you do these things?"

Chris rose, stretched and then in the most leisurely way imaginable, began to tap out an answer. It was short and to the point. "I'm a smart dog." Indeed he was! Hitchings stared at the canine in disbelief. What did they have here? He had admired Chris and marveled at his abilities, those remarkable gifts that he and his fellow scientists seemed to know so little about. But a dog that could, in effect, talk? That was almost too much to contemplate.

After that, a good deal of information passed between the dog and his human interrogators. They learned among other things that Chris had been aware of his unusual abilities since the age of two and had just been waiting for an opportunity to practice them. He also noted that he, in common with humans, learned by doing and that he was now able to do much more complex mental tasks than he had when his talents were first recognized.

Once they could communicate with Chris, the investigators naturally hoped that they might begin to unravel all the secrets of the canine identity and perhaps much of what remained unknown about the animal world in general. Sadly enough, this did not prove to be the case. The dog's thoughts seemed strangely confined to the present or near present. He could remember little of his past and seemed to have no communication at all with other animals, including dogs. His attention seemed almost wholly directed to the human world. It was, as one scientist noted with a shudder, almost as though Chris were a human and not a dog.

Whatever the case, Chris's fame spread. He was examined by teams of experts from such prestigious institutions as Duke and Rhode Island universities. Many of the investigators were naturally suspicious of his abilities and came prepared to refute them. They could not. The dog was simply what he was. His powers, though remarkable, were not unique; for horses, cats and other dogs have been known to manifest similar characteristics. Though at present no satisfactory explanation for such phenomena has been offered.

And he had something else in common with certain of these animals. Like them, he was a prophet. The unfortunate Uncle Harry had discovered this, and inevitably others were bound to also. It all started with the weather. One of the investigators, noting the sullen look to a certain day in late summer, remarked idly to Chris that it "looked like rain." To his astonishment, the dog responded that it would not rain that day or the next. In fact, it would not rain for four days. One can imagine the interest with which the scientists observed the passing of the next four days.

Of course, it didn't rain, but that could have been just a coincidence; so the investigators set other tests for Chris: Would the state legislature raise the annual budget? Would the local favorites win their next baseball game? How many pups would the dog next door have? And, no, the dog wasn't always right; but he had an astonishingly high percentage of success, far higher, in fact, than could be attained by any form of random selection. Clearly the animal had some form of clairvoyant power.

To just what extent Chris could tell the future was never fully determined, however; for the following winter the dog suddenly began to lose—or perhaps abandon—his remarkable gifts. Quite without warning or any signs of accompanying ill health or other cause, Chris gradually began to withdraw from human contact. Perhaps he had simply gotten tired of communicating with people. Whatever the cause, he first stopped doing computations; then, at last, he refused to make further predictions.

It was a great disappointment to the scientists, of course, but to Johnny it was a relief. Chris was his dog again. They could talk together (with Johnny doing all the talking!), run, play and explore. The good old days had returned.

But before giving up this last skill, the dog left a final legacy to mark his great achievement. When asked one day if he knew when he would die, he responded (in 1959) that he would expire on June 10, 1962.

For the next three years Chris's life was so normal, so typically canine, in fact, that the Andersons could hardly believe that their pet had for a brief period been a great mathematician and remarkable prophet. But then Chris died, and his death, after a long, full life, brought his powers once more vividly to mind; for he expired on June 9, 1962. He had been wrong by but a single day!